THIRTEEN TALES OF TEXTUAL AROUSAL

First Edition

Published by The Nazca Plains Corporation
Las Vegas, Nevada
2010

ISBN: 978-1-61098-021-0
E-book: 978-1-61098-022-7

Published by

The Nazca Plains Corporation ®
4640 Paradise Rd, Suite 141
Las Vegas NV 89109-8000

PUBLISHER'S NOTE
Thirteen Tales of Textual Arousal is a work of fiction created wholly by *Robin Anderson's* imagination. All characters are fictional and any resemblance to any persons living or deceased is purely by accident. No portion of this book reflects any real person or events.

Cover, Blake Stephens
Art Director, Blake Stephens

DEDICATION

For PB and TT
(Peter Burton and Torsten 'Tasty' Højer)
Per me, meglio del Carnivale di Venezia!
(For me, more fun than the Carnival of Venice!)

THIRTEEN TALES OF TEXTUAL AROUSAL

First Edition

Robin Anderson

CONTENTS

CONTENTS CONTINUED...

NO STONES AGAINST
MY WINDOW

Not only was Nathan Bartholomew known as a beautiful young man, Nathan Bartholomew was, in fact, exquisite. Tall, blond and with piercing azure blue eyes, his much admired frame – more sinewy than muscular – was usurped by a spectacular and formidable penis. Following in the family tradition of all former male Bartholomews – a pompous line of Colonels and Brigadiers – Nathan was doomed to follow in their booted footsteps. After his initial training and on achieving the more humble status of mere Second Lieutenant, Nathan was modestly despatched to Afghanistan. In his equally more humble status as a mere off-duty soldier and whilst being in the wrong place at the wrong time, the exquisite Nathan Bartholomew was inadvertently – but spectacularly   blown up.

Achilles Court is one of those severe, unattractive thirties blocks of flats in a quiet street close to Ennismore Gardens in London's exclusive Knightsbridge. Flat 1a on the ground floor had been extensively adapted for the needs of the reclusive, mysterious Mr Bartholomew who, apart from the daily visit by Andrew – his carer – lived alone. From vague observations passed on by Fred, the aged porter, the flat remained in perpetual gloom aided and abetted by permanently closed, dark louvred shutters to all windows and the equally dark panelled walls throughout. Lighting, kept to the absolute minimum would only allow the very occasional visitor – Nathan's lawyer or doctor – to make out the vague shape of their host as he sat, heavily shadowed, in his electrically motorised wheelchair.

A sudden intrusive shaft of light through an errant louvre or slat could offer a quick glimpse of a gnarled, claw-like hand – the right hand missing the index fingers and its two adjacent companions – had, according to the agog Fred, 'quite done me gut in!' However, the permanently agog Fred had been unable to offer any more to this gut-wrenching experience, the left hand having remained in shadow as had the rest of the former, exquisite Nathan.

Every morning the carer would wash and clean his patient, dressing him in his de rigueur outfit of loose tracksuit bottoms, a loose, long sleeved buttoned shirt and soft, well-worn velvet monogrammed slippers (Nathan's only indulgence), his crippled feet resting askew on the platform support of the wheelchair. Nathan's breath was raspy and nasal with a permanent soft, wet bubbling noise from the gaping nasal cavities, the cartilage and flesh having been burned away. Surprisingly, his former melodious tenor voice had remained unimpaired. On his insistence – apart from his long sojourn in a hospital specialising in trauma and burns where he had lain like a mummy swathed in bandages – his devastated parents were, never again, to be received by their once perfect son.

'Remember me as I was,' he would whisper into the telephone when speaking to his softly weeping mother. 'Please just remember me as I was.'

Reading and music were Nathan's only pleasure; food had been reduced to a basic necessity with all food served in a liquidised form prepared daily by the vigilant but hypocritical Andrew. Conversation between him and the carer was nothing more than monosyllabic; the same with Fred. Only Nathan's doctor and accountant had the privilege of being allowed the rarity of complete sentences.

Ironically, the only salvaged part of Nathan's nigh-on-cremated body had been his gigantic penis and a pair of loosely hanging pendulous testicles. His penis, like a long, thick, pale heavily ribbed sock hung heavily against the deep, drooping, swagged scrotal sack. To his twisted – and insatiable – almost hourly delight, the tortured young man had discovered the uninhibited pleasure achieved by gripping his vast shaft which, when erect, fitted firmly between his disfigured thumb and little finger. Up, down, left, right, twisted, turned, squeezed and pinched and with the thick, juicy, folded foreskin pulled backwards and forwards there was – pun not intended – no holding Nathan.

Andrew, his awestruck carer, would repeatedly regale his equally awestruck partner with vivid details of his employer's prowess. 'Honestly

Derr (short for Derrick), I don't know where it all comes from though, when you see the size of those bollocks of his… Christ, yer talkin' about a pair of fuckin' tennis balls 'ere!'

The gawking Derr would listen rapturously at the descriptions of Nathan's daily dozen and more. 'Christ, the globules of cum I have to clean up! Off his bloody feet, off his sodding wheelchair, off the fuckin' floor! Just as well the whole fuckin' flat is that Amtico stuff and easy to wipe clean!'

Because of being confined perpetually to a wheelchair Nathan had insisted on faux wooden floors throughout the apartment.

And Derr's only memorable comment apropos his partner's endless dissertations as to his employer's prowess? The cryptic 'Maybe he should open a sperm bank to go hand in hand with his wank bank!'

'Nathan? David, David Lowles, your old school chum. At last I've managed to trace you! How the hell are you?'

A stunned silence. 'David Lowles?' Nathan could barely hide the astonishment – nor the fury – in his voice. 'How the fuck did you find me? No, let me re-fucking rephrase that. Which shitty fuck of a cunt gave you this number?'

A reciprocal stunned silence greeted this mini tirade before the hurt voice tentatively replied. 'Jesus, Nate, it's David. Your soul mate from school.'

'I know exactly who you are!' retorted Nathan, his nostrils dribbling wetly down to the burnt opening and exposed teeth representing his mouth. Yes, he thought venomously. David Lowles, the doppelgänger to Michelangelo's whore! The prick tease and cock tease combination of all time. Flaunting yourself at us – in your eyes – lesser mortals. Us – to quote you – queers! Aware of all those mind fucks desperately wanking off around you whilst you, you arrogant turd, simply went off into the proverbial sunset and shagged Mellisa Meyerling, Miss Super Fuck of St Augustine's for Girls. And the rest!

On the other end of the silent line, David Lowles was similarly thinking. What's happened Nate? I've been told you've been somewhat badly wounded and confined to a wheelchair but you're alive and that's the most important thing. Oh shit! A thought flashed through his mind. Don't tell me he's still pissed off about that Catherine fiasco? Christ, she is so of the past and so unimportant. Yes, that's it. Silly bugger! I bet it's all about little old Cath! Smiling into the receiver, he said, 'Right! Now you've got over the shock of this blast from the past, when are we going to meet?'

'I don't see people,' came the snapped response accompanied by the strange bubbling, gurgling sound. 'Ever!' The last utterance being followed by the dialling tone.

'Well, fuck you too, Nate,' replied David looking down at the silent instrument in his big hand. 'Two can play at this game.' He checked a piece of paper on the desk in front of him and dialled another number. 'Mrs Bartholomew? David Lowles. I spoke to Nathan but it wasn't at all successful, I'm afraid.'

'Oh David, dear David,' came the tremulous reply, 'I did try to warn you it would be of no use. Even Gwen, his favourite cousin, has tried but he refuses to see anyone.' There came a soft sob. 'And he totally refuses to see me…his mother…' The sobs began to grow in volume. 'His own mother!'

'Shall I simply drop by? A surprise visit as it if were?'

David's sudden suggestion caused the woman to stop mid sob. 'Oh dear, I don't think so, David.' There was a long pause. 'I don't know how to tell you this but Nathan…Well, David, Nathan…Nathan, he's so disfigured!' The last word came out in a slurped sob. 'Even though I'm his mother, I have to say it…he's…he's horrible!' Mrs Bartholomew now burst into a hysterical sobbing. 'Oh, forgive me,' she finally managed to gasp. 'But it's so unfair, David! It's so unfair as to what's happened to him and even more unfair that he was allowed to live!'

Two days later David, having been given the address but strongly advised by a hesitant Mrs Bartholomew to only visit when Andrew the carer would be able to let him in, tentatively pressed the buzzer to No 1a, Achilles Court.

TEN YEARS EARLIER

'Nate, you old dog, you! Don't tell me you've actually taken the plunge and asked the ice maiden out?' David, his voice more amused than incredulous, gave his friend a lewd wink. 'Tell you what, if you even manage to touch a tit – be careful you don't get frostbite! – drinks are on me!' He gave another laugh. 'Tell you what, to oil that previously unexplored tunnel of love, why don't you two have drinks beforehand with the lovely Melissa and *moi?* We can meet at Melissa's place – her folks are away for the weekend – and have a few drinks there. More intimate than the Hind, if you catch my drift?' (The reference being made to the Hind pub where the publican, Albert, an old queen who openly slathered over David and his dark, matinee-idol looks as opposed to Nathan's more blond Pre-Raphaelite appearance, was always prepared to turn a blind but lecherous eye with regard to these two underage drinkers.)

'I don't think so, Dave.' Nathan gave an uncomfortable laugh. 'Melissa? Well, she's a bit OTT for a girl like Catherine. Another time perhaps, after I've gotten to know her more.'

'You mean after you've fucked her!' David gave a crude chortle at his friend's obvious embarrassment. Teasing Nathan and his attempts to pass as 'straight' always amused the other teenage boy. I know you'd much prefer me to be fucking you, my friend, David thought mischievously, but that would be like attempting to blow Bin Laden! You haven't a hope in hell!

'Only joking!' he said instead. 'Only joking.' Aware of his friend's obvious embarrassment he added quickly. 'OK, OK, a brief drink at the Hind. Besides Melissa and self are on planning to see the new Russell Crowe, Gladiator, which means you two can go on and do whatever you had planned.' David could not resist another snigger. 'Hopefully our Russell the Muscle will be more entertaining than, er… your Catherine of Arrogant!'

'Oh, fuck off, Dave! That's not even remotely funny.' Nathan stood up from where the two had been sitting in their local Starbucks. He glared down at his grinning friend. 'At times you can really push it, can't you?' His face infused with anguish he added, 'That was uncalled for and unkind.' His face flushing furiously Nathan went on to whisper. 'You know – unlike you – I've never been with a girl and as my best friend you should be a bit more sympathetic. Not all of us a rampant rams like yourself. Some of us need more time.'

'I can't say you're selling yourself short, Nate.' David couldn't resist a snigger. 'Let's face it with that cock of yours it would be an impossibility! No… don't interrupt! I – and the whole school – would give an arm or a leg for half of what hangs between your legs so don't waste it!'

Nathan continued to stare down at David, his face now a deeper crimson than before. 'My cock has nothing to do with it.' He hissed. 'Nothing! I simply have some principles as opposed to being nothing more than a heartless fuck machine.'

'Heartless fuck machine? Is that how you see me?' David, his own temper now rising, could not resist the final barb. 'Pity my fuck machine doesn't swing both ways! Should it ever, I bet you wouldn't refer to me – and it – as heartless!'

Nathan's look of fury changed to one of abject horror. 'Why on earth made you say that?' He managed to croak. 'Are you saying I'm gay? Or, in your words, queer?'

'Oh Nate, oh Nate,' said David placatingly, knowing that he had now gone too far. 'Forget it! No, I don't think you're gay, queer, a poofter, shirt lifter, fudge packer or whatever you want to call it. I'm only teasing because you just... well, you're just taking so fucking long to get laid. You're sixteen for Christ's sake!'

Nathan gave his friend a long, cold stare. 'The Hind, at four.' Without a second glass he turned on his heel and walked out of the coffee bar.

'See you there,' muttered David to the empty doorway. He gave a wry smile before getting up to fetch himself another mug of coffee. This could be fun, he thought as he stood waiting to be served. Forget Melissa, I'll get Nate and the Catholic cunt Catherine pissed and stoned then fuck her in front of him knowing all the time he will be gagging to be the one on the receiving end! David couldn't resist a snigger and muttering out loud – much to the consternation of an elderly pair of grey-haired matrons – 'I've never done it up the arse even with the fuck heap Melissa so, maybe I'll just try it with you, Nate, while Miss Catholic cunt watches and sees what else she's been missing!'

Nathan and Catherine Noble ('That name simply has to be a joke!' David had quipped after their first introduction) were already seated at a corner table in the Hind, their drinks in front of them. Catherine's, an orange juice with a splash of vodka and Nathan's, a Coca Cola with a healthy dollop of brandy, had been promptly served by the leering Albert. Catherine had boldly accepted Nathan's whispered suggestion of 'a sharpener' and sat giggling nervously at her daring. Nathan, even more nervous than his virginal date, had simply swallowed his drink in a few noisy gulps resulting in a rapid return trip to the bar counter.

'So, where's that dishy Dave, then?' whispered Albert throatily, his thin tongue flicking lasciviously between his continuously moisturised lips. He nodded his bony chin in the direction of the softly giggling Catherine. 'What are you doing with her?'

'She's my date for the evening,' said Nathan defensively. 'We're going on to The Troubadour for dinner afterwards.'

'Your date?' Albert raised a badly plucked eyebrow. 'I thought dishy Dave was always your date.'

'David is not gay!' retorted Nathan crossly, 'And well you know it!'

'Well, why waste your time then is what I always say,' retorted Albert, more camply than crossly. 'Either get it or forget it! And, speaking of "getting it," yer straight friend has just arrived!'

David, having given a quick glance around the nigh on empty room, gave a friendly wave and made his way over to Nathan and a leering Albert. 'Sorry I'm late,' he announced with a dazzling smile. 'Bit of a bird problem.

Miss Melissa is unable to join us. Woman troubles, I believe.' He gave Albert a sly nudge across the counter top. 'At least she's not preggers, though – after the last couple of shags I gave her – she ought to be having fucking quads!' What he didn't confess to was a blazing row between the two of them with Melissa refusing to be seen out 'with that stuck up constipated cow' and screaming at David to 'fuck off then!' on him being adamant that the four should meet.

'We're over there,' said Nathan picking up his glass. 'Maybe you'll join us after you've finished enthralling Albert with your latest tales of conquest.'

'He's just nervous,' smiled David leaning conspiratorially across the bar. Putting his mouth close to an ecstatic Albert's ear, he hissed. 'Tonight's to be his first time with a bird and that's the sacrificial hen!' David gave a snigger at his wit while Albert gave a high pitched squeal of evil delight. Pouring a triple brandy into David's glass of Coca Cola, he whispered, 'This one's on me on condition you come back and tell me all!'

'Melissa sends her apologies, Catherine,' said David smilingly as he sat down opposite the decidedly flushed girl. 'She was so looking forward to meeting you properly but, as she says, she's sure there'll be another time.' He pointed to her empty glass. 'Same again?'

A giggling Catherine nodded shyly. 'Yes please,' she whispered. Like most of the girls in her group David Lowles was the teen idol to end all idols. A combination of Daniel Radcliffe (sans glasses) and Orlando Bloom plus his charm and devil-may-care attitude, to be a friend of David – never mind the exalted status of girlfriend! – was considered the ultimate accolade. Yes, Nathan was good looking but good looking to the extent of being beautiful and therefore not quite manly enough. Most of the girls assumed Nathan was gay and Catherine, on being asked out, had agreed quite happily for – as she had confided to her best friend Belinda – 'I know there won't be any hanky panky!'

'Three more please Albert and one for yourself?'

'Oh thank you David,' said Albert prissily.'A Baby Cham would be perfect!' He gave another quick flick of his slippery tongue. 'Triples?'

'For them, not for me. I'll have a plain Coke.' David paid for the drinks including barman's faux champagne, adding, 'You haven't seen this,' before slipping a Rohypnol tablet into the vodka and orange. As a quick afterthought he snapped a second tablet in half before slipping the smaller portion into Nathan's glass.

'I feel strange,' murmured Catherine. 'In fact, I don't feel at all well.' She gave Nathan a wild-eyed look to be greeted by a slack-eyed gaze in return.

'Me too…' muttered Nathan. 'Shit, how much brandy was there in these drinks?'

'What you both need,' said David brightly, 'is something to eat! Come on! Chop! Chop! I've got my Mum's car outside – she doesn't know as she and the old man are out for the evening! – and we can call in and get a takeaway somewhere. I have the keys to a mate's flat in Redcliffe Square where we can – with his blessing – party as well as make full use of his well stocked bar.'

'No party… I wanna go home…' were Catherine's last words before she slumped out in the passenger seat of the car, her head resting against the headrest.

'Jesus Dave!' Nathan, struggling for words leaned forward from the back seat where he too had slumped. 'Those drinks… what the fuck did you put in those drinks?'

'A little something to help you get rid of your first night nerves,' laughed his companion. 'And look, here we are. Now, out you get, Nate and, if you can, give me a hand with getting this sad sack of shit into the flat.'

Catherine was dumped unceremoniously on the bed of the small but luxurious flat. 'Right,' said David, turning to look at Nathan who was leaning precariously against the door jamb, his head lolling dangerously. 'There she is, Nate. All yours. Ripe for the plucking or, better still, ripe for the fucking! So, out with that yardstick of yours and break her in with a fucking she'll never forget!' He gave another snigger. 'Shit! With the Rohypnol she's swallowed, make that never remember!'

'You drugged us?' Nathan's voice came out more of a strangled squawk than a question.

'Only the cunt, not you, Nate. Well, not you entirely. Let's say you've been given a slight tranquiliser to calm your nerves but not your cock.' He gave a laugh. 'So, what are you waiting for?'

David stood staring at the bewildered-looking young man now gripping onto the door jamb for all his worth. 'Ah, I forgot. Maybe you're not quite sure what to do, well, here's the next best thing. Watch and learn!'

Without hesitation David, kicked off his loafers, tore off his pants and underpants and, smiling broadly at his stunned friend, lifted the moaning Catherine's skirt before pulling down her tights.

'No condom for me.' laughed David, 'And as she's no doubt going to be tight, tight, the more fun with the friction of breaking her in!' David, his own formidable cock now angrily erect, scrambled onto the bed. Callously kneeing the girl's legs apart and, with a further glance over his shoulder to the now sobbing Nathan, he crudely thrust himself completely and deeply into the compliant girl. Drug or no drug Catherine's reaction was immediate. With a loud shriek she began to scream and writhe under the energetic young man's relentless pounding. David, in his excitement and unable to muffle the now hysterical screaming simply punched the girl as hard as he could in the face. With a soft sigh she fell silent as a frenzied David, piston-like, thrust and thrust again into her bleeding cavity. 'Liking what you're seeing and missing Nate?' David glanced over his shoulder only to see Nathan now cowering against the wall and weeping softly. 'Oh shit!' cursed David before giving out a loud groan and shuddering in a series of heaving spasms as he came. 'Oh shit, Nate! Come on, it's your turn! This is what we're here for!'

'Nooooo!' The animal-like cry caused David to pull himself out of the supine girl, his still erect cock glistening in a covering of blood and cum. 'Nooooo!' came the cry again. 'Why her? Why not meeee?'

'You want me to fuck you?' David couldn't resist a snort of laughter. 'Right into my hands, pretty pansy boy Nate! As I said, I'm not usually an arse bandit and I've never done it with a guy but, what the hell! Why not for Christ's sake? Keeping it in the family as if it were.'

Having cleaned himself up in the en suite bathroom David went through to the small sitting room where poured himself a strong brandy. Having taken several fortifying gulps he made his way back to the bedroom, his erection once again beginning to assert itself. 'Oh for fuck's sake, Nate,' he said to the figure now lying huddled in foetal position on the carpet. 'Get a grip! Either you want to be fucked or you don't. If so, get those pants off, push the bitch aside and get onto the fucking bed!'

Several minutes beforehand a sobbing Nathan, clinging to David's naked legs, had declared his undying love and desire for his friend.

'Fuck me! Do what you want with me, Dave! I love you! I want to suck you! I want you inside me! I want to be yours forever!' had been only a few of the whimpered pleadings coming from the drunken and semi-drugged young man.

As if in slow motion David did as requested and, for the second time that night, had to rinse a mixture of blood and cum from his now somewhat tender cock.

THE PRESENT. ACHILLES COURT.

'Who the fuck's that?' Nathan turned his shadowed head in the direction of the muffled sound of the entry buzzer coming from the front hall to the flat.

Andrew, clutching Nathan's freshly wiped well-worn monogrammed slippers in one hand, a scented face cloth in the other – he had just wiped his employer's feet with the cloth having completed giving him his blanket bath – looked at Nathan with genuine puzzlement. 'I have no idea, sir. It could be a delivery or perhaps someone visiting another flat may have pressed your number by mistake.'

'Go sort it out,' grizzled Nathan, 'and then bring me another Bloody Mary and a fresh straw. This one, like your whole fucking attitude, is soggy!'

'Of course sir – and I'll fucking well spit in it,' muttered the small man under his breath as he made his way daintily through the small hallway to the front door. Still muttering to himself he peered into the small entry screen. 'If it wasn't for the extortionate amount of money your misguided mother pays me, I'd be off. Another year then Derr and I will be able to open our B and B in Brighton and so up yours, you crippled monstrosity! Hel-lo!' he added, still speaking sotto voce as he stood transfixed by the handsome face peering intensely up from the small black and white screen. 'And who may you be who's come a calling?' Andrew clicked onto the intercom. 'Hello?' he cooed, in his most refined manner. 'May we help you?'

'Mr Bartholomew please.' Before Andrew could respond – the little man was completely taken aback as he was convinced the buzzing had been in error – the handsome face broke into a smile. 'It's an old friend and I want to surprise him! I take it that's Andrew I'm speaking to?'

'Yes indeed! Andrew it is, sir!' simpered the elderly carer.

'Well Andrew, my name's David Lowles. Mrs Bartholomew gave me this address – plus your name – so I could pay a surprise visit. Knowing how difficult Mr Nathan can be about visitors, Mrs Bartholomew and I thought it a cracking idea if you just let me in and let me announce myself.'

'Well, er… I don't know, sir,' stammered Andrew. 'He really never sees anyone. Not even his parents.'

'I know that Andrew,' said the still smiling face. 'But, this is a very special visit and he will be delighted I can assure you.' The smile broadened. 'Mrs Bartholomew also tells me you and your friend are great balletomanes.' The smile became even wider, if possible. 'It just so happens that I have two best seats in the grand tier for the royal gala in a week's time with Edward Watson making one of his rare appearances.'

'Edward Watson!' The little man's voice came out with a mouse-like squeak. 'Oh sir! Well, don't say I didn't warn you about Mr Nathan and his temper!' Andrew buzzed David in.

'What is it?' called Nathan hoarsely from the shadowy room. 'What the fuck are you playing at, Andrew?'

'Oh, it's a surprise delivery!' carolled the little man airily. 'I won't be a mo, Mr Nate!'

'Well, hurry up, you moron. You've still got my fucking slippers and where's that fucking drink?'

'Quietly now,' whispered David placing his forefinger mischievously to his lips. 'Just as well you were here, Andrew.' He handed the flustered carer an envelope. 'Your tickets.' He gave another whisper. 'Had you not answered the door I was just about to throw a pebble to two against that large shuttered window to the left of the main entry doors. I take it that is the main room?'

'Oh yes indeed, sir!' Andrew gave a girlish, derogative titter. 'What a lovely thought. As I repeatedly joke with Mr Nathan, with ancient me it's definitely a case of no stones against my window!'

'Nonsense, Andrew!' said David snidely. 'Why, if for some reason your long standing partner couldn't get you to answer a few stones it would. without a doubt, be followed by a boulder!'

'Oh sir!' squeaked the delighted carer again. He pointed to the darkened doorway. 'He's in there.' He whispered.

'For fuck's sake Andrew. Where the hell are you and bring me my fucking slippers!' Nathan's voice came out in a low, strangulated gurgle of fury. 'Get in here at once, you fucking little toad!'

'You called sir?' David, having taken the pair of slippers from Andrew, stood silhouetted against the dimly lit doorway to the hall.

A stunned silence greeted the camp intonation followed by a whispered, 'Who the fuck are you?'

'The person you last you told you never saw people, ever! Nate' – David gave an uncomfortable laugh. The heavily scented figure sitting in the shadows was certainly disconcerting. 'It's me! David! You must have known I wouldn't take no for an answer and so here I am.' He gave another nervous laugh. 'I even come bearing gifts in the form of your slippers!'

Expecting an explosive 'Fuck off' or a 'Get the fuck out of here' David was subjected to a silence broken only by the laboured, gurgling breathing of the shadowy form. Finally, unable to stand the tension a moment longer he moved tentatively forward. 'Well at least let me put on your slippers for you.' The silence grew heavier and more ominous. Hesitating for the briefest moment David moved forward and, with a graceful bend knelt in front of the dimly illuminated wheel chair, his eyes riveted by the scarred, skeletal, crippled, twisted feet resting at odd angles on their platform. 'Jesus, Nate,' he whispered, tears springing to his eyes. 'I had no idea...'

'Grotesque, aren't they?' The well-remembered voice came throbbing from above his bowed head, the bubbling sounds now reduced to a minimum. 'Pitiful, aren't they? And that's for starters!' There was another silence as David got slowly to his feet. 'Oh, I'm hideous alright, David Lowles.' The voice, though still low and vibrant now took on a more strained tone. 'So, may I ask why you're here? Not to apologise for raping Catherine and me that night are you? Surprised I mention this, Dave?' Nathan gave a burbling snort. 'You left me to deal with Catherine that night. You changed hers and my life forever, Dave. Were you aware of that? You drop me a note saying you were leaving for the States and would keep in touch. Frightened Cath was going to the police were you? Or even me? What a cowardly shit you were that night and still are no doubt though coming to see me must have taken some guts. Or was it to gloat? Yes, was it to gloat, Dave? Ten years later you reappear! Some friend. Some keeping in touch.' There was another snort. 'Yes Dave, you did that night what I always had wanted you to do. Fuck me. But I wanted you to fuck me out of friendship, if not out of love. Christ! You didn't have to drug me, nor did you have to rape poor Catherine to prove your fucking point.'

There was another soft, throaty laugh. 'You certainly wouldn't want to drug me now, Dave, that I can tell you. In fact, there isn't a hallucinatory drug strong enough to make you even able to touch me, never mind look at me.'

'I was quite prepared to put on your slippers for you, Nate,' David said softly.

'I have Andrew for that,' said the voice from the shadows. 'I'd like you to leave now, please. Ask Andrew to see you out and Dave, please don't come back.'

David stood looking at the figure in the chair. 'If that's what you want, Nate.'

'It's exactly what I want, Dave. Now please go.'

Slowly David turned and made his way to the door.

'Oh, and Dave?'

'Yes Nate?'

'Before you go there's a light switch on your left. Flick it on and take a long last look at what you fucked that night out of sheer vindictiveness and petty spite.'

'I don't think I want to, Nate.' Came the nervous reply.

'Of course not! How remiss of me to forget what a fucking coward you were and therefore still must be.' Gurgled Nathan. 'Put on the fucking light!' He roared.

David slowly turned to face the figure in the now brightly lit room. Expecting the worse he was still completely unprepared for what he saw in front of him. What could only be described as a blackened mummified skeleton dressed in a pair of track suit bottoms and a loose fitting shirt showing a pair of virtual fingerless hands, sat huddled in the wheelchair. The only mesmerising items were the bright, piercing azure blue eyes and the enormous, ludicrously disproportioned lumps and tubular length nestling between Nathan's emaciated thighs.

'Hello, lover!' croaked the figure.

Clutching at his mouth David rushed into the hallway where a solicitously prepared Andrew was standing alongside the open door to the lavatory. Falling to his knees for the second time within the last ten minute David vomited copiously. Having rinsed his mouth and splashed his face with cold water, David re-entered the hallway.

'Sorry about that, Andrew.' He said sheepishly.

'I know sir,' smiled the little man gently. 'It's just I'm now so used to poor Mr Nathan that I don't even see him as you must have.' He handed David his coat. 'You'd better leave now sir and I'd better go and attend to Mr Nathan.' Andrew gave a wry smile. 'I have a feeling I'm going to have quite a difficult day once you've left.'

'For the second time, Andrew, I'm sorry.'

'Forget it sir. And,' here he gave David a coquettish smile. 'Thank you again for the tickets. Derr and I are going to have such a posh time!'

'Good! And Andrew,' David took a card from his jacket pocket. 'Just in case... here's my card.'

'Thank you, sir. I'll leave it on the small tray on the hall table here.' He gave a small giggle as he looked at the tray. 'Until today, sir, it was a case of no cards upon my calling tray!'

'Andrew, all I am going to say is don't you ever let anyone apart from my two regular visitors into the flat again.' There was an embarrassed silence. 'What did he say to you out there after he was so elegantly sick?'

'Nothing much, sir. However, he did leave his card on the off chance you may wish to see him again?'

'Who knows?' Nathan gave a throaty gurgle. 'Maybe, if given another chance, this time he won't throw up!'

'Quite, sir,' agreed Andrew, giving in to a small smile of triumph.

Back in the gloom Nathan had fumbled for the telephone. Laboriously punching in a number he waited for the phone to be answered. Without any introduction he simply said, 'I need your assistance.'

Three days later the body of David Lowles was discovered in his Mayfair flat by his elderly cleaning lady. The body had been viciously stabbed – the pathologist would go on to count forty seven stab wounds – but only after David had been tied spread eagled across the four poster bed and viciously and obscenely raped. Such was the violence of the rape that David's anus had been left torn and bleeding. To add a final insult to the scenario a large stone had been found deeply wedged inside David's completely destroyed anal passage.

That same evening an excited Andrew and Derr sat proudly in their prime seats alongside the royal box where a smug Prince Charles and the horsey Duchess of Cornwall sat chatting affectedly with their equally as smug guests.

To add an extra sense of panache to their evening, Andrew had hired a limousine to collect them from their small terrace house off Munster Road in Fulham. The same limousine would be taking the pair on to the Ritz where a romantic dinner had been planned. After that it would be the night bus back to reality.

'It's a funny old life,' Andrew had mused as the elegant Mercedes had purred its sleek way toward the West End. 'Here we are hobnobbing with royalty tonight and there's poor Mr Nathan sitting alone in all that gloom with nothing, but nothing to look forward to.'

'Even funnier what you told me about him this morning,' lisped Derr, brushing aside a troublesome bleached lock from his lightly bronzed forehead.

'Yes, wasn't it,' agreed Andrew, his small old face taking on a puzzled expression. 'I still cannot work it out how, instead of wearing his slippers as he usually does when he decides to spend the night watching a film or two and then sleeping in his chair – he wouldn't let me put him to bed as per usual when I left – I found him wearing trainers this morning.' He gave a camp laugh. 'I didn't even know he had any trainers, never mind wore them. Furthermore, I could have sworn they bore traces of what looked to me like what must have been old blood stains. Never mind, just another mystery connected to the flat of horrors. Oh my, Derr! Look! We're here.'

Derr let out a camp giggle. 'Now, no waving you silly old queen, leave that to the real McCoy!'

DASHING AWAY WITH
THE SMOOTHING IRON

Jennifer stood solemnly watching Mrs Thomas as she expertly finished ironing one of her father's pristine white shirts, folding this into its final perfect folds and, with a satisfying hiss of steam, pressed the hot iron once more onto the immaculate fabric.

'There,' she said, smiling down at the pretty little six year old. 'Another chore completed!' Placing the ironed shirt deftly onto a nearby pile she looked affectionately at the blonde, blue-eyed 'little angel' as she called the child when describing her to Mavis Denning, her neighbour. 'Proper little angel she is, is that Jenny. Like a little Shirley Temple. And she's so excited at the thought of a new baby brother!'

Mrs Harbourd, Jennifer's mother, had been taken to St Mary's, Paddington, by an excited Mr Harbourd earlier that morning.

'Your new baby brother should be home within a few days, Jenny poppet,' her doting father had told her on his return. 'Like you, we are all so excited at meeting him. I'm sure Ronnie (Mr and Mrs Harbourd had insisted on knowing the sex of their new child) will be equally as excited at meeting his big sister Jenny!'

'Big sister Jenny!' Jennifer liked the sound. Smiling proudly at her father, her big blue eyes wide open in wonder at the thought of a baby brother, the little girl had echoed the words, 'Big sister Jennifer.' Thrilled at the sound of this new phrase she repeated the three words time and time again to herself in the form of a silent mantra.

Having made this announcement Mr Harbourd had given the beaming little girl a light kiss on her forehead before returning to the screams and shrieks of his wife as she strained and pushed to bring the aforesaid new baby brother into the world.

Jennifer looked at the small bundle with more curiosity than her anticipated feeling of sisterly devotion. In her child's mind she had envisaged a pink, smiling, cooing doll-like perfection as opposed to the wrinkled, red-faced, bald thing wrapped up in a blue cashmere blanket and being proffered to her by her proud, smiling parents.

'He's ugly,' said Jennifer.

'No, he's not!' reprimanded Mrs Harbourd with an indulgent smile. 'He's beautiful and he's Mummy and Daddy's new precious!'

Had Mrs Harbourd been watching her daughter instead of ogling her new offspring yawning in her husband's arms, she would have caught the quick look of panic crossing the little girl's face.

Jennifer's mind was racing. New precious? But she was Mummy and Daddy's precious. Not this ugly intruder! As if reading her thoughts, Ronnie began to howl. The howling – better described as more of a high pitched yowling – was to continue intermittently for the next few hours. To Jennifer's chagrin, instead of being put out by the baby's loud crying, both Mr and Mrs Harbourd simply went on 'oohing' and 'aahing' and talking to the screaming bundle in idiotic baby talk.

The little girl was even more mortified when some of this baby talk was inadvertently applied to her!

Her! Jennifer! Had her parents suddenly forgotten that she was a whole six years old? Not only that but – even more importantly – had they also forgotten in so short a space of time she had now taken on the important role as this hideous little thing's Big Sister?

The next, even greater shock, was seeing her new baby brother's even more hideous little thing itself! This occurred a week or two later when Agnes, the new Scottish nanny specially employed to take care of the new arrival, asked Jennifer if she would like to help her 'bathe baby Ronnie.'

Agnes – highly recommended by a friend of Mrs Harbourd – had quickly assured both the parents that she would take full control in handling 'the wee bairn' while keeping an eye on the little girl as well (up until now Jennifer had been happily cared for by the doting Mrs Denning). Mrs Harbourd's wonderment at her achievement of the birth was short lived as was the novelty of the noisy, new arrival. She was now much more interested in getting her figure back to its former, wafer-thin shape and returning to her hectic social activities than dealing with a new baby. And furthermore, as she had said to her now equally disenchanted husband, Jennifer's involvement in helping Agnes with the new baby could only be a good thing. 'Can only help them in bonding together!' she had trilled airily to her spouse.

It should be noted that Ronnie had been conceived with some reluctance. It was only due to her husband's persistent insistence on a son 'to take over the business' (Mr Harbourd owned a successful chain of second hand car dealerships) that Mrs Harbourd had suffered the appalling indignities of childbirth for a second time. Jennifer's scan had been acceptable – little girls were pretty and adorable – but, as she had insisted from day one, a nasty, smelly little boy was to be her husband's – and a nanny's – responsibility.

'What's that?' asked Jennifer, pointing at the strange, acorn-like appendage poking up from between Ronnie's plump legs.

'That's Ronnie's pee pee,' said Agnes briskly. In no uncertain terms she went on. 'Surely someone – Mrs Thomas or mummy – must have told you, dear, little boys have pee pee pipes and little girls have wee wee holes? It's how God made them.'

'Has daddy got a pee pee then? Even though he's a big boy?'

'Yes, of course, dear.' Agnes couldn't believe her ears. How could a child have reached the age of six and yet still be so innocent?

'As funny and as tiny as Ronnie's?'

'No, dear, I'm sure not,' said Agnes, colouring slightly. 'I'm sure your daddy's is a bit bigger.'

'Will he show it to me if I ask him?'

'I shouldn't think so, dear. Daddies only show their pee pees to mummies!'

'Does daddy show his pee pee to Mrs Thomas then?'

'Oh, no dear!' exclaimed Agnes looking distinctly shocked. 'She's a housekeeper!'

'But she's also a mummy! She's got two nasty sons, Ted and Tim. They use naughty words like fuck and they smell!'

'Please don't use that word, dear,' said Agnes faintly. Gathering herself together she added brightly, 'And although Mrs Thomas is a mummy I am sure your daddy has never, ever shown Mrs Thomas his pee pee!'

'Shall I ask him?'

'No, dear! Definitely not! Now, no more talk about pee pees. Here,' she handed the now scowling little girl a towel, 'Help me dry Ronnie's little toes. Gently dear, gently…'

Jennifer took one of the tiny, chubby feet in her tiny hand and, unbeknown to a now softly humming Agnes busily patting the upper part of the baby dry, she gave a tiny toe the biggest pinch she could muster. Sitting back on her heels with a sweet smile on her pretty little face, Jennifer listened with increasing satisfaction and an inner delight as Ronnie's screams reached an unprecedented decibel level!

Agnes looked at the baby in alarm before rising to her feet, clutching the yelling, kicking child to her ample bosoms. 'What did you do, child?' she cried. 'What did you do to him?'

'Nothing, Agnes! Nothing! Oh…' Jennifer's pretty little face began to crumple. 'You think I'd hurt my new baby brother?' Now it was time for her tears to flow. 'You're wicked, Agnes. Nasty like Ted and Tim! I saw you squeeze him too hard! You hurt him, not me!' Drawing herself to her full height she suddenly screamed up at the startled nurse, 'I'm going to tell Mummy on you and Daddy too!' With a choking sob she had gone dashing from the nursery bathroom.

A shocked Agnes found herself dismissed later the same evening and ordered to be out of the house with all her belongings by the next morning. Throughout the angry discussion leading up to her dismissal Agnes vehemently denied having deliberately squeezed the baby too hard. The woman almost fainted at the next accusation that she had also traumatised their little daughter by pulling on Ronnie's foreskin to show how much further his little penis would grow and, by using her index finger as an extra addition to the stretched little member, had shown how it would grow even longer.

Mr Harbourd, in particular, was incensed, particularly at Jennifer's whispered confession that Agnes had told his little daughter he 'had a big one' and why couldn't she be shown it as he, her daddy, had 'shown it' to Mrs Thomas.

'Your daughter's lying! Lying!' Agnes had cried in self defence. 'She's making the whole thing up! Your daughter's a little monster in the making!'

'Jennifer never lies!' snapped Mrs Harbourd in reply and that was that.

Mrs Thomas, with her usual cool-headedness and common sense, promptly came to the rescue, offering her niece, Sharon to step in and take over Ronnie's welfare until a new nurse could be found. The agency, alarmed by Mr and Mrs Harbourd's claims, had said they would be dealing with the disgraced Agnes 'in the proper manner' and a replacement would be found 'tout de suite!' To the relief of the agency's head, the use of such a stylish phrasing had the immediate desired and calming effect on the claimants.

Jennifer was completely dazzled by the gum chewing, foul mouthed Sharon. The teenager, with her carefree, slap dash attitude had immediately told the star struck child that she'd be a nanny to Ronnie but a 'friend' to the little girl. 'We're exactly alike,' she told the awed Jennifer. 'As pretty as hell and as naughty as a cage full of monkeys!'

Nor was Jennifer the only member of the household to fall under the Sharon Smith spell, so did an equally dazzled Mr Harbourd. However, in his case it was decidedly more lust than love.

Whilst his wife remained cool, aloof, fashion conscious and very sparing in her allowance of 'you know what' (as she delicately put it) Sharon literally lived, breathed and smelt of sex. Her disregard for the de rigueur white nanny's overall saw her sashaying around the house in the skimpiest of cotton tank tops and the briefest of skirts instead. Added to these were a pair of precarious platform shoes plus a pair of anklet chains, all of which contributed to Mr Harbourd's growing desires and wanting. There was no question about it, he simply had to f-u-c-k Sharon!

The dirty, devious deed unexpectedly took place the following weekend with Mrs Harbourd and a girl friend taking themselves off to Paris for a weekend's shopping. 'Maddy and I'll be at the Ritz, darling, should you need to call.' She had said, giving her husband a tight, artificial smile. 'However I'm sure the children will be more than enough to keep you occupied!'

Sharon, no novice to the intricacies and shenanigans of sex (she'd already fucked two of her three brothers and her Uncle Dick), was well aware of Mr Harbourd's interest. An extra sway of her hips, an extra pout plus the added cock-tease of bending over without bending her knees when picking up the odd scattered toy thus giving Mr H – as she now called him – a glimpse of her panties, were all part of her daily fun.

Came the first evening of his wife's departure and after much deliberation – plus several large whiskies in the privacy of his study – the enamoured man, first having taken a bottle of white wine from the small fridge kept in the room – nervously entered the kitchen where the young girl was busy fixing Ronnie's bottle. A beaming Jennifer, in between eyeing her idol adoringly, was busily tucking into a plate of verboten fried sausages and chips, a half finished Coca Cola, in lieu of the usual glass of milk, next to her plate.

'Er… I was just about to open a bottle,' said the man giving out a forced laugh. 'Would you care to join me for a glass?' He gave another decidedly nervous guffaw. 'I take it you are old enough to drink alcohol?'

'Oh yes, Mr H!' pouted the girl, nodding her bleached blonde head reassuringly. 'I've even been pissed several times!'

'Well, that's alright then!' laughed Mr Harbourd self-consciously, eyeing Jennifer who had stopped eating and was watching the two with an innate curiosity. Averting her eyes from her father's anxious glance *her* glance just happened to settle on an enormous bulge which seemed to be growing mysteriously out from the front to her father's trousers. (Mr Harbourd, as part of his usual routine had, on returning from the office, taken a shower and changed into his usual T-shirt and loose cotton chinos but without the obligatory underpants. Unless, of course, Mrs Harbourd had made other arranagements).

Sharon too could not help but notice the impressive, still developing, bulge.

'I'd better sit down,' said Mr Harbourd, abruptly doing so. Like his daughter and the young girl he too had become acutely aware of his massive erection. He gestured weakly towards the bottle of wine. 'It's been a long day and I'm pooped. Would you mind fetching the corkscrew and a couple of glasses, please Sharon?'

As this little scenario was taking place Jennifer's tiny mind was racing. Daddy's pee pee seemed to be growing and growing, but why? For once the little girl decided not to expound on her curiosity.

Sharon and Mr Harbourd ('call me Andrew!') quickly made their way through the first bottle of Pinot Grigio, the silent, staring Jennifer being completely ignored. 'I'll go and get another bottle,' muttered the besotted man. Suddenly noticing the scowling child (Jennifer's star struck look had slowly changed from one extreme to the other) he said brusquely, 'Oh, Jenny! Shouldn't you be in bed?'

'I'll just help Jennifer to bed and look in on the baby and then I'll be back,' cooed Sharon. 'And you'd better make sure you're still here on my return, Andrew!' she added archly, her eyelids fluttering in what she considered a vampish look. The last remark being accompanied by a thrusting forward of her ample breasts, the nipples pressing blatantly against the thin cotton of her tank top.

Mr Harbourd gave a gulp. 'As if I wouldn't be,' he managed to croak.

Several hours later the little girl, unable to sleep, heard her whispering Daddy and a giggling Sharon sneaking past her bedroom door. Her curiosity once more aroused Jennifer lay under her Rupert Bear decorated duvet, straining her ears for any other sounds. What were Daddy and Sharon doing? Unable to resist the temptation Jennifer finally roused herself from her tiny bed and, having cautiously opened her bedroom door, tiptoed quietly along the deeply carpeted corridor towards her parents' bedroom. She was aware that Sharon's room was up a further flight of stairs and she was quite sure she hadn't heard her going up these.

Reaching the heavy white panelled door she pressed her tiny ear against the cool wood, her eyes widening at the strange filtered sounds of groaning, panting and muffled squeaks plus yelps coming from the room. Frowning and with a concerned and determined expression on her pretty little face, Jennifer slowly opened the door. Standing in absolute silence she absorbed the scene taking place in front of her in a mixture of fascination and horror.

Daddy was positioned above a whimpering, squeaking Sharon, his pale bum jumping up and down, whereas Sharon's plump legs were wrapped around his middle, her anklet bracelets jingling where her ankles crossed and met behind his hairy back. More alarming was that as Daddy's bum jumped up Jennifer could see his thing, his enormous pee pee coming half way out of the noisy girl's wee wee before he pushed his thing back in again, causing Sharon to give an even louder yelp. As the open-mouthed little girl continued to watch, Daddy's bum began bouncing higher and higher and faster and faster and just when Jennifer was convinced he was about to push Sharon through the mattress, Mr Harbourd began to groan, writhe and wriggle on top of the equally acrobatic Sharon. With a final yell followed by a bellowed 'Fucking hell!' Daddy then collapsed right on top her!

After all was said and done, Jennifer still saw Sharon as her friend and there, in front of her very eyes, Daddy had not only stabbed her repeatedly with his huge, ugly pee pee but had also squashed her! Giving a small whimper the little girl withdrew from the doorway, closing the door gently after her. Standing in the dark corridor, deliberating as to her next move, she heard Ronnie beginning to howl. To both her relief and alarm Jennifer heard Sharon's faint, muffled voice through the now closed door. 'Oh shit! I'd better go and see to the little bugger!'

'Don't stay too long!' Came her father's playful reply. 'Old One Eye here is already getting his second wind!'

'Dirty bastard!' Giggled Sharon. 'I won't be long!'

Quickly Jennifer drew herself back into the deeper shadows of a nearby doorway just as a stark naked Sharon came hurrying through. The little girl stared after the disappearing figure. No, she thought in a growing fury. Sharon wasn't hurt, Daddy wasn't angry and what was even more bewildering, Sharon was going back for even more of what they were doing!

The betrayal was immense. If it hadn't been for Ronnie she wouldn't have met Sharon and if it wasn't for Daddy doing things with his revolting pee pee, Sharon would still be her friend. But most of all, if it hadn't been for Ronnie she would have still been Mummy and Daddy's precious and therefore Sharon would not have been an intrusion in their otherwise perfect lives.

There was only one solution. With an extra-determined look on her perfect, angelic face, the little girl made her way back to a room adjacent to the master bedroom suite. The room, with doors both to the master bedroom and the corridor, had been turned into a lavish dressing room for her parents, complete with a permanently set up ironing board, clothes press and three walls of 'his' and 'hers' cupboard space.

Ronnie's screams eventually subsiding, Jennifer finally heard Sharon making her way back to the main bedroom. Now fully alert the little girl heard the teenager's teasing voice. 'Wakey, wakey, sleepy head! You and One Eye have work to do!'

Jennifer waited for what seemed an eternity before creeping back to the now closed, thickly panelled bedroom door. Once again she was subjected to the sounds of moans, groans and panting working their way to a muffled crescendo. 'Now!' the little girl muttered to herself before scampering back into the dressing room where she picked up the previously turned on steam iron standing upright and ready on the ironing board.

Carrying the iron in front of herself with both hands she scurried along to the nursery, nudging open the half-closed door and rapidly approaching the silent cot. Without hesitation but with a quickly hissed 'You did this!' she raised her arms small arms above the cot railings and, leaning over these, placed the scorching hot iron onto the sleeping, blanketed bundle. A rewarding smell of burning fabric accompanied by a rapid burst of smoke along with the most horrendous shrieks and screams from Ronnie proved even more edifying than she had possibly imagined.

Within seconds a panicking Sharon burst into the nursery with Jennifer quickly slamming the door closed behind her, thus blocking out Sharon's bewildered gasps of 'Oh my God! Oh my God! What's happened? What's happened?' being heard along the main corridor.

'What the...?' A wide-eyed Sharon turned from the scorched, smoking now silent bundle in the foul smelling cot only to see a small fury still clutching the iron, glaring up at her. 'Jen...' she began to say, reaching out a shaking hand but the teenager – in a state of almost catatonic shock – was a fraction too late. With a high pitched cry of rage the little girl leapt forward wielding up all the power she could muster in her tiny frame. Hefting the heavy iron towards the terror-stricken teenager Jennifer caught her a crushing blow full in the face. Without uttering even the smallest of sounds Sharon sank slowly down onto the tiled floor.

Little Jennifer, however, was not yet through with the punishment of her traitorous ex-friend. Opening the nursery door – she was half expecting her father to call out to see if everything was alright – she gave a small sigh of relief at the overwhelming silence. Daddy had more than likely dozed off again. Closing the door the little girl re-entered the room, and stepping around the prostrate Sharon, made her way over to the small night light glowing alongside the cot. Unplugging the lamp she quickly inserted the plug for the iron into the socket. Seconds later she pressed the 'Steam' button, the iron giving out a satisfying hiss and jet of scalding steam.

With a look of utter concentration on her small face, her tiny tongue sticking out through her rosebud-like little mouth, Jennifer slowly pressed and repressed Sharon's face repeating the same process up and down her body. Sitting back on her heels the little girl observed her handiwork with approval. Sharon had been steamed to a perfect lobster red, her skin now hideously blistered and peeling. A highlight of the whole procedure had been when Jennifer switched from 'Steam' to 'Iron.' Placing the red hot iron on the alarmingly bushy mound of hair between Sharon's thighs had resulted in the hair being sizzled to a crumbling crisp.

'Now Daddy,' said the little girl to the two steamed and scorched bodies (she had also given Ronnie a neat pressing and toasted his unsightly, nasty little thing). Making sure the iron was as hot as it would ever be she walked boldly up to the master bedroom. Somehow, even in her panicked exit Sharon must have closed the door, hence the reason for her father's apparent lack of concern at the noises coming from the nursery. Placing the iron carefully down on the floor, Jennifer quietly opened the door and silently entered the darkened room where her father lay naked on his back, snoring gently. Peering at his supine figure, the little girl could not resist a small giggle at the sight of the long, flaccid penis lying worm-like against a pale, hairy thigh.

Without further ado Jennifer simply – as she later told the friendly police lady – 'put the iron on my Daddy's pee pee and pressed the steam button.'

Daddy survived the ordeal but never to be a complete man again. Mummy divorced Daddy on the grounds of his infidelity (his inability was tactfully not mentioned in the proceedings) and Jennifer, after some expensive counselling, was allowed to return to live with Mummy. The trauma inflicted upon the innocent little girl by her wicked, cruel father, thus leading to her momentary mental instability had seen Jennifer become the darling of the press while dastardly Daddy became a pariah.

Mummy quickly married again.

Much to Mummy's annoyance and her new Daddy's delight, Jennifer was once again blessed with a new baby brother.

THE THIRTEENTH PARTY

Paulo Roderiguez smirked at the reflection in the long mirror. 'Yes!'
He muttered to himself, his voice low, coarse and guttural. 'Now you are one
handsome bastard!' His smirk became even more self-satisfied – if possible
– as he surveyed his head of thick, wavy dark hair, his large 'come-to-bed'
brown eyes, his aquiline nose plus his fine moustache and beard.

Paulo secretly saw himself as a dynamic, dashing more twenty
first as opposed to seventeenth century version of the 'Laughing Cavalier',
by the Dutchman Frans Hals; a perfect melding – in his eyes – of George
Clooney and Orlando Bloom as opposed to the plump, smirking, self-
satisfied moustachioed rake in the famous portrait.

His eyes dropped to his torso; a muscular perfection, smooth and
tanned, a teasing line of thick, crisp, dark curly hair leading down from
the neat, dimpled belly button to a heavy-headed, pendulous uncircumcised
penis nestling against a dark, equally pendulous sac containing a pair of
spectacular balls.

His legs – the thighs well defined, the calves muscular but not too
bulky and a pair of elegant, tanned feet – completed the tableau of male
perfection.

'All I can say again,' remarked Paulo, the smirk now replaced by a
lascivious grin of gleaming white teeth, 'One seriously handsome bastard!'

The true reflection, a reflection to which Paulo, in his overwhelmingly blind arrogance (and therefore also ignorance) was completely unaware, presented a very different portrait. The mirror, in reality, showed a head of thick, oily not-too-clean hair, small, piggy-like eyes, slightly squint and clinging closely alongside a thick, fleshy nose which terminated in an alarmingly bulbous end.

A brave, straggling but determined moustache could not hide the thin, chapped lips and an equally straggly beard failed dismally in its attempt to disguise a weak receding chin. In fact, what the dimly lit, slivered mirror truly revealed in its honest reflection was a melding of Heironymous Bosch meets Francis Bacon – a nightmarish combination – as opposed to the aforesaid gods of the other silver screen!

Paulo's torso, a flabby combination of slightly pendulous pectorals and the definite swelling of a starving, Biafran-like belly was further ridiculed by a thin, caterpillar-like trail of hair leading down to a long, thin penis topped by a rancid foreskin. A pair of shrunken balls – reminiscent of two dried figs – dangled coyly behind the scrawny appendage. His legs, a pair of pale shanks with a smattering of dark hairs ended in a pair of bony feet, the toenails horny and yellowed with the toes themselves not-too-clean.

The grin accompanying this self-satisfying observation displayed a set of teeth seriously in need of a heartless, ruthless dental hygienist. To Paulo they remained a dazzling parade with the proud owner oblivious to a differentiation between the tones of gleaming white and dulled pewter.

Paulo, at his own choosing, found himself a loner. Regarding his college contemporaries as either 'oiks' or 'oafs' he saw himself strutting alone in similar vein – to quote the treacherous Cassius from Shakespeare's Julius Caesar – 'like a Colussus' – and the aforesaid fellow students as 'petty men' whom – in his fertile imaginings – were worthy of nothing more than to 'walk under his huge legs and peep about.' Needless to say, the dislike was reciprocal. Paulo's companion students – likewise in the second year of studying at the college – saw him as nothing more that a disgusting 'fucking faggot' who one day would get his 'come-uppance' and that day would be sooner than later.

The term 'fucking faggot' had evolved mainly from Paulo's unfortunate less attractive blessings by a cruel Mother Nature plus the hero-worship bestowed upon him by the college's very obvious and therefore token 'fag' or 'gay,' a frail, effeminate, quiet, intelligent and studious blond boy with the additional humiliation of the name Rock, cast upon him by a mother obsessed by the former movie star of the fifties and sixties, Rock Hudson. The fact that Hudson had died of AIDS added grist to this unfortunate mill with the poor boy being subjected to taunts of 'Show us yer cock, Rock!' and 'Like it up the bum, chum?' or the even more derogatory 'Piss off cunt! Better rejected than us infected!' The latter taunt was usually delivered by Doug Williams, a large, hefty good-looking twenty year old studying business management along with Paulo, who epitomised the terms 'oik' and 'oaf' but, to the surprise of all his lecturers, sported a formidable brain. (Doug would go on to become a successful business man making a killing in the world of property wheeling and dealing).

Rock's whole world had changed one Friday afternoon when he had paid a necessary visit to the toilet adjacent to the local library. At the start of a weekend the library was usually a silent haven with only a few elderly regulars, a few layabouts who had come in for the sake of a few snatched moments of warmth plus one or two disenchanted librarians. Rock's main purpose had been to scour the reference section for more information on one of his more favourite subjects, the French writer Jean Genet (Rock had aspirations of writing a searching novel himself about the agonies and loneliness of his own childhood. The teenager saw his main character as a martyr to what he deemed, his 'affliction,' and doomed to a tragic end).

Slipping into an empty cubicle – even though the urinal stand was empty Rock was continually on the alert in case someone else would come in and stand nearby – the privacy offered by the small enclosed space was preferable. In the past jibes such as 'Show us your cock, Rock ' or 'Watch your cocks, lads, the cock sucker is here!' had led to the teenager rushing out of the toilet, still dribbling into his hastily zipped-up pants and almost in tears. Although he was now in a public toilet as opposed to a school one, old habits died hard. Having just sat down on the seat – he preferred to sit even when having a pee – the young man was aware of a strange muffled panting sound coming from the adjacent cubicle. Even in his haste to relieve himself Rock had noticed the door to this particular cubicle being semi-closed and had automatically raced into the open one. The panting and shuffling sounds turned into what could only be described as an alarming series of groans. Not knowing what to do and concerned by the sounds of someone who was obviously in pain or trouble, Rock offered out a tentative 'Are you alright in there?'

A deafening silence greeted the question.

Rock's alarm grew tenfold. Had the subject of the painful noises finally collapsed? Hastily pulling up his underpants and trousers – and yes, still dribbling! – Rock pulled open his own door and pushed open the door to the next cubicle.

'What the fuck…!' A startled red-faced Paulo, his pants and underpants in a tangle around his ankles, glared up from where he was seated, his cock still jerking spasmodically in his hand, a messy festoon of translucent cum oozing from between his fingers.

'Oh!' was all the flabbergasted Rock could say, his eyes riveted by the still jumping midget cock, the immediate comparison to that of a small angry carrot flashing through his mind. 'I thought you were having a fit or something...' he added lamely.

'No, not a fit! A wank!' snapped Paulo, wiping his cum-covered hand across his sparsely decorated chin. 'And what the fuck are you doing in here anyway?'

'Having a piss and not a wank!' said Rock boldly, his eyes still riveted to the defiantly erect cock. 'Er...you're still hard!' he added for want of something to say.

Paulo gave him a beady look. Although he had never joined in with the slagging off of the pretty young man standing in front, Paulo was immediately aware of Rock's open intrigue by the unexpected scene confronting him. He was also aware that an equally scathing was quickly required to counteract the 'Having a piss and not a wank' crack.

'Yes,' said Paulo in his best, sinister voice. 'Have you got a problem with that?'

Rock swallowed audibly, his shapely, girlish mouth trembling. 'No...er, Paulo.'

Paulo narrowed his eyes. Although not the least bit gay he had heard of straight blokes allowing gays to give them a blow job – after all, it wasn't like proper sex with full penetration and all that – and here was a gay guy obviously fascinated by his monster dick so why not. After all, nobody would ever know. 'You want to get down here and suck it? See if you can make me come again?'

Rock gulped more loudly. 'I've er...never sucked a cock before,' he whispered, his eyes widening and shining with growing excitement, his own penis beginning to press against the front of his pants.

'Well,' laughed Paulo, in his best 'man of the world' manner, 'There's always a first time.'

Without any further hesitation Rock dropped to his knees. Within seconds he was gagging and choking on Paulo's second explosion of hot, acrid cum. 'Jesus!' The wide-eyed young man stared down at the still bobbing, sucking and slurping blond head. 'Jesus! For a beginner you're fucking A!'

If the truth be known, Paulo had never been given a blow job before but, as the popular adage reasserts itself time and time again, 'There's no going back.' Having roughly asked an instantly besotted Rock for his telephone number (who ever said 'love is blind' would have found the perfect example in Rock's then and there bolt of love lightning!) Paulo called him on the Saturday and again on the Sunday. The two ensuing clandestine meetings took place at the lavish Roderiguez family home inside a rose festooned summer house, beneath the myriad climbing blossoms and among tubs of colourful, staked rose bushes. The summer house, set conveniently towards the back of the substantial garden attached to a large, rambling detached mock Tudor horror set in one of the city's more affluent outer suburbs, provided an ideal venue for these secret assignations.

Carlos Roderiguez, Paulo's overweight, overbearing and over indulgent father – the same affections being showered upon his comely wife – was the proud owner of a highly successful import company dealing wholly with best quality beef and roses coming in from the Argentine. Even the fracas over the Falklands had done little to diminish the welfare of the business, the majority of 'loyal' Brits being more gourmet than government orientated.

Rita Roderiguez, Paulo's definitely overweight but exquisitely dressed, manicured and coiffed mother, inspired by the success of the roses imported by the family concern had taken to growing and developing her own blooms with an almost religious fervour. As a result of her endeavours the woman was the proud winner of several prestigious rosettes for her tall, elaborate blooms grown in regimented tubs in a large greenhouse adjacent to the summer house. Each rose bush, inspired by the regimented precision in which they were displayed, stood proudly upright tied to their special wood carved stakes (made from the finest of imported hardwoods). Rita Roderiguez would skittishly refer to the specially turned stakes as being the stakes to her 'many hearts!' – a camp referral to the heady blossoms.

However, no rose could compete with the proud mother's ultimate 'heart,' her son and heir, the repellent Paulo.

On numerous occasions she would repeat in hushed tones of absolute awe, 'But it's my baby boy, Paulo, my son, who is the one and only true stake through my heart.' The bewildered recipient to the horrendous apparition responsible for such a denouement would simply nod dumbly in response or stand there shocked rigid into deafening silence (rather like Mrs Roderiguez's roses!).

On Sunday evening, a panting Paulo, his cock well-lubricated with his own foul smelling spit, viciously fucked a sobbing, groaning, ecstatic Rock. If the recipient of Paulo's vicious carrot had been besotted after giving his lover both their first blow jobs, the feeling went into overdrive. Besotted became obsession.

While Paulo chose to ignore the devoted, dewy-eyed Rock should they have ever met on the college premises, his paramour was not so discreet.

To Paulo's embarrassment he was now forever being subject to waves of recognition and cries of, 'Hi Paulo! Good morning! Afternoon or evening! On one or two occasions there had been a sniggered, 'Rock's got the hots for Quasimodo!' (this from a smirking Doug to his cohorts) or 'The princess has found her frog' from Julie Marr, a vivacious red head, one of the many girls who hung around Doug and his gang of cronies. Doug and Julie were considered an 'item' and it was a known fact that they were always 'doing it' whenever circumstances gave them a chance. It was Julie who announced to the Doug Brigade, as the set prided themselves on being, that only a blind person would not be able to see that Rock the Cock and Quasi in their turn, were 'an item.'

Until the Rock and Paulo scenario, Julie's malicious eye and scathing tongue had been previously vindictively at work elsewhere.

Titania Delevine smiled coquettishly at the reflection in the full length, gilt-edged mirror. 'You'll do,' she whispered to herself in her high, eloquent girlish voice. 'Whoever catches your eye tonight will be one very, very lucky young man!'

She pursed her lightly tinted rosebud-shaped mouth, her left cheek dimpling prettily. Her light blue eyes sparkled almost as brightly as her elegant Theo Fennell gold chain necklace featuring a heavy, diamond encrusted cross, which hung seductively between her neat, not too big and yet not too small breasts. Her cocktail dress, a flurry of pale blue chiffon by hallowed designer Charles Svingholm, enhanced her eyes to perfection.

Her peaches and cream complexion, with just the hint of a stolen kiss by some flattering shaft of sunlight, added an infused golden glow to the dazzling vision she was surveying with such obvious delight. But Titania could not stop there. She went on to look appraisingly at the petite waist, the elegant arms and the long, shapely legs encase in shimmering silk. Pale blue satin shoes by Jimmy Choo gave an extra lift and enhancement to the already shapely calves. A wicked anklet chain (in reality a diamond bracelet from the aforesaid Theo Fennell) acted intoxicatingly as an illicit, discreet inhalation of cocaine.

'Good girls,' according to Titania's equally self-satisfied group of similarly self-indulgent friends did not wear ankle chains, nor did 'good girls' do Charlie. At least not – according to all the 'good girls' in her 'groupette' – in front of the parental nor public eye.

'The glamour of Cameron Diaz meets the sophistication of a young Grace Kelley,' Titantia acknowledged out loud to the silent mirror. She gave herself a gracious, almost regal nod, her soft blonde, shoulder length hair rippling gently. 'Miss Titania Delevine, even though I have to say it myself, you are exquisite!' She gave a winsome smile, displaying a perfect set of pretty, pearl-like teeth.

The true reflection, a reflection to which Titania, in her overwhelmingly blind arrogance (and therefore also ignorance) was completely unaware, presented a very different portrait. The mirror showed a head of thin, brittle, over-streaked hair, small washed out watery blue eyes (she refused or wear contact lenses or glasses), a nose starved of cartilage and reminiscent of a lopsided hook and a small, thin mouth representing a mini hyphen under her wide nostrils.

What the mirror was also seeing was a melding of Ugly Betty meets Edvard Munch, a truly nightmarish troglodyte and a self-induced scream. Titania's figure, a scrawny, pale combination involving a pair of undeveloped, putty tipped breasts superimposed on a bony rib carriage and an unfortunately thick waist, led down to a pair of legs that would have been more appropriate on Chicken Little. Along with her defiant ankle bracelet Titania had also daringly shaved her pubes leaving a garish gash which would have made Lizzie Borden proud!

The extravagant blue satin Jimmy Choo shoes were more Minnie Mouse than Minnie Driver, Titania – like Cinderella's ugly step sisters – having been cursed with a gravity-defying pair of extra large feet. 'But,' as the vision had said on more than one occasion, 'Whereas Beckham has made bunions beautiful, I make statuesque sublime!' The smile accompanying her self-deliberations showed a set of teeth seriously in need of a callous orthodontist. To Titania these remained a glowing string of pearls with the proud owner oblivious to the differentiation between pearls and putrefaction.

'I always thought Tired Tits and Quasimodo would get it together,' Julie would wickedly repeat to the amused Brigade. 'That would be a pure coupling made in Hell.'

Doug's remarks were more basic. 'Look over there, Quasi not coming to the aids of the party!' (This when an irritated Paulo was seen angrily trying to fob off Rock who would be eagerly waiting outside one of his lecture classes to talk to him). Or more often than not, the more vindictive, 'Rock the cock who sixty nines Paulo the schlock!'

The more observant Julie would take it even one step further. 'Titania Tired Tits is too busy with her own fairy ring to notice the charms of Quasi.' Julie was convinced Titania was 'a lezzie.' She would often say to her own giggling coterie, 'Nobody, but nobody, could ever fuck that, never mind even think of it! Why, I bet she and that Tracy Sharp do more than simply study the same humanities course. Inhumanities is more like it!'

To which her grinning paramour would add evilly time and time again. 'If you want my honest opinion the two of them are nothing more than a pair of fuckin' muff munchers!'

The sniggered terms 'the sixty niners' and 'the muff munchers' had become de rigueur when discussing the group. What Julie and her gang failed to recognise was Titania's nigh-on-obsession with Doug and her extreme dislike for Julie and her cronies. If the truth be known, Titania had never ever seen Paulo around the college nor was she aware of Rock's own existence. Keeping herself to herself, the young woman had not even confided her suppressed feelings to Dorothy Simpson, her supposedly best friend. Dorothy and her circle in turn only tolerated Titania because of her social standing, her father, Hugo, being a Member of Parliament and her mother, Diana, a member of the extremely wealthy Corbay family who owned – so rumour had it – several acres of prime real estate in the City as well as having taking a shrewd gamble by buying – 'on spec' – even more acreage in the desolate East End areas of London before the official site of the new Olympic City site had finally been decided upon. Diana Delevine, inheriting her grandfather's active business brain had also started a conglomerate of highly successful estate agencies.

The Delevine mansion in Chester Square was host to many extravagant parties at which Titania presided like some aloof queen. To date she had not approached Doug about attending one of these future events but tonight was the night. Titania was going to a birthday party given by one of her mother's friends for her own daughter, a plain, sullen girl named Elizabeth Watson, whose only claim to fame was the family money plus her own, surprising development as an up-and-coming horsewoman. Added to this was her supposedly torrid affair with her riding instructor, an ex-Olympic champion whose extra mural activities also supplied him with a substantial extra income. One of these 'suppliers' coincidently just happened to be a Mrs Henrietta Watson, Elizabeth's mother, who generously sponsored the instructor's clandestine income in addition the her daughter's extortionate fees.

Armed with the knowledge Doug Williams was to be a guest (rumour had it that he too was part of Elizabeth's 'riding' set) saw the invitation more of a challenge than a chore. This was the night that Doug Williams was going to be made very aware of the presence of a certain Miss Tatania Delevine. A slight problem was the foregone conclusion that the jarring Julie would also be present. The date, Saturday the thirteenth, she saw more as auspicious as opposed to suspicious. Titania had been born on a thirteenth herself and therefore considered the number (and her mother!) extremely blessed.

By the time Titania arrived, the party – an extravagant birthday 'do' given by her mother's friend for her daughter in the ballroom of a prestigious Knightsbridge hotel – was in full swing. To her satisfaction the young woman noted what could only be taken as envious glances at her appearance. Yes, tonight was to be the night when she would snare her prince, albeit the loutish Doug. But what a catch, what a prince and what a feather in her cap!

Mrs Watson had done her daughter proud. The mysterious Mr Watson (away somewhere making money) was not present for the gracious occasion but raffish Sean Byers, the handsome riding instructor was there, in his role as an uncomfortable substitute. The priapic young man had been made to energetically 'ride' his hostess prior to the event, much to the chagrin of her daughter who stood scowling alongside the two greeting the excited arrivals. A harassed Sean had whispered hurriedly to the jealous girl that he'd be giving her 'a shag to remember later' but the hasty promise had done little to soften her mood. Even when the handsome stud had asked her for a dance she had remained coolly aloof, her mood only changing when the irritated young man had hissed angrily in her ear in the midst of a turn, 'Well fuck you, sweetheart, your ma's available if you aren't!' Within seconds Elizabeth changed from frigid to frivolous.

To Titania's puzzlement – and delight – Julie appeared not to be present (she had been invited to Paris for a weekend's shopping by her bored and neurotic mother) which meant 'Operation Doug' could be put into action more easily than anticipated. Choosing a moment when Doug was standing by himself at the long bar table waiting to be served, she undulated her way (shuffled) over to him.

'Why, heeello!' she cooed, fluttering her eyelashes demurely.

'Huh?' Doug, giving a start, turned round and peered down at the fright standing alongside him. Jesus fucking Christ, he thought wildly, not Titania Tired Tits! What the fuck is she doing even attempting to talk to me? Instead he managed to mumble, 'Er…hello Tits er…Titania. Great party, isn't it.' A desperate statement, not a question.

Titania made no reply but continued gazing up at the handsome, thuggish young man with what she considered her most seductive, vampish look.

Doug looked wildly around the crowded room of laughing young people before catching the eye of Matt Thomas, his best mate, standing chatting with the group of cronies he had just left. Matt, on catching Doug's wide-eyed expression of almost camp horror, gave a lewd chuckle and followed by an even lewder gesture, moving his tongue in and out against his bulging cheek.

Grabbing a proffered glass of wine with relief Doug offered the still ogling young woman a weak smile. Christ, what gives with this cunt? If she flaps those fucking eyelashes anymore she'll almost be giving me a terrestrial blow job. His broad grin at his joke gave Titania the chance she had been waiting far.

'Has anybody ever told you you have the most enigmatic smile?' she tittered coquettishley. 'Or should that be pragmatic?'

'Huh?'

'And yes, I'd simply lurve a drinkie!'

'Oh shit! Er…yes, well I'm sure the barman will help you.' Doug gave a panic stricken glance back at his now openly laughing group of friends. 'Must go. See ya!' With a half hearted gesture in the form of a toast he quickly made his way back to the group of young men, only to be greeted with a series of ribald comments and sly innuendos, 'Tired Tits after the Dougmobile, huh?' or 'Jesus, the poor bitch is just dying for our Doug to do her Douggie fashion!', Julie's constant reference to Titania's so-called lesbian leanings being momentarily overlooked.

'Take a fucking pack of hounds to fucking satisfy that uncracked cunt!' snarled Doug with a man-of –the-word smirk, little realising how prophetic his words were to be.

'Poor young man!' tittered Titania to herself as she reached for a flute of champagne. 'So shy and yet so very interested! Look at the sweet thing! No doubt he's boasting about being acknowledged – at long last – by the tantalising Titania Delevine!' Taking a dainty sip of her drink (more of a slurp than a sip) she tossed back her sparse hair in a madcap, carefree way. Tonight's going to be fun with a capital F! She thought crudely. 'Naughty, naughty wench!' she uttered out loud, startling a passing Mrs Watson.

'What, dear?' The officious woman stopped in midstride, her arm firmly clamped to that of a leering Sean.

'Oh! Er nothing, Mrs Watson! Nothing at all. Simply saying to myself it'll be an absolute wrench when one has to leave such a heavenly party!'

'Oh? Why thank you dear!' Giving Titania a tight smile (surgically enhanced) the woman stalked on before turning round to give the young girl another curious look. Turning her head back she leaned up towards her stud whispering something into his ear. Giving out a roar of appreciative laughter Sean Byers turned round to stare at the now red-faced Titania. Seeing her perplexed expression he promptly gave her a broad wink, causing the butt of their humour to flush an even darker shade of red.

'Common bastard,' muttered Titania. 'Mother and daughter's paid fuck.' Brushing down the panels of her blue chiffon dress (even Charles

Svinghom's brilliant endeavour was beginning to look both wilted and defeated), she shuffled ungracefully back toward the bar where she demanded a champagne cocktail, 'And don't stint on the brandy!'

Another loud guffaw from Douglas's group of baying friends caused Titania to glance surreptitiously in their direction. Yes, they were looking at her and no doubt thinking what fun she was and how lucky Doug was to have been lucky enough to have been subjected to a few, charitable seconds of her time. Giving the group what she considered a seductive, languorous look, she downed her extra strong cocktail in a single, triumphant swallow before holding the glass out for a replacement.

'She's knocking it back!' observed another of the group dryly.

'If you had to look at that apparition in a mirror, wouldn't you?' joked another.

'Not if I was shit faced! Jesus, imagine seeing two of that?'

More laughter followed the comment.

'Fucking hell!' cried Jasper Crippen, a spotty fourth year medical student. 'Imagine two sets of those tired apologies for a pair of tits dancing in front of you? More like two sets of used condoms than a happy handful!'

More ribald laughter.

'What car did you bring?' The sudden question from Doug caused Spotty to give a small start. 'Why?' he asked. 'The V70. I always drive this.'

Doug nodded in the direction of the now obviously very drunk Titania who had remained at the bar, trying to give the impression of being mysterious and aloof whereas now her whole demeanour was one of a person about to collapse. 'I have an idea and if you're all game, let's teach the bitch a lesson. She's gagging for it.'

Paulo, on one of the few occasions he would reluctantly allow himself to be seen out in public with his paramour, had finally agreed to go along with Rock to the small, luxurious cinema based alongside the hotel in which Elizabeth Watson's birthday party was, at that moment, reaching its drunken and noisy crescendo.

'The film was crap!' snarled Paulo as they walked past the uniformed doorman and on towards a small mews where he had parked the car. 'As I told you after reading those ridiculous reviews, why glamorize one of Isherwood's most glorious, seedy characters and worse still, why put him in a glass house when he wallowed, yes, absolutely wallowed in both a dump and self pity!'

'Well, I liked it and I thought Colin Firth was fantastic!'

'Well you would, wouldn't you?' snorted Paulo before adding cruelly. 'After all, he too is a member – like your gender member doppelgänger Miss Hudson – of the silver screen.'

'Oh fuck off, Paulo!' chided Rock crossly, his attention momentarily caught by some activity and loud cries of drunken mirth from the direction of the cars parked in the dark, tree shrouded cul-de-sac adjacent to a large, silent, brooding church. 'That sort of comment doesn't become you!'

'No? Well, how about this one? Rock does not mean the hardness of your cock; softie!' (Rock was particularly self-conscious that, unlike his lover's rampant, angry, fiery coloured carrot his semi-flaccid puny, pale slug-like appendage was never going to win an Oscar).

'Oh, piss off!' With an angry flounce and tossing of his long blond forelock, Rock minced off into the direction of a nearby mews where Paulo had parked his car.

Paulo gave the departing figure an exasperated look. Their squabbles were becoming more and more frequent and Paulo, who had on more than one occasion found sexual solace elsewhere – Jimmy Carruthers, the school water polo star the surprising, willing substitute. Jimmy, with his almost indescribable, sordid fascination – still to be discovered and explored by a naive Paulo – had immediately picked up the scent that the surly student held all the potential of developing into willing and able 'scat scum' partner. Though they had as yet to practise the 'other ultimate intimacy' as Jimmy vaguely described it – Paulo was curious to hear more! – time for 'testing the turd' was imminent with Jimmy planning to squat and squit above the willing or unwilling Paulo sooner than later.

The young swimming star's other hidden vice was an extravagant dependency on cocaine with his main supplier being a dubious West Indian boasting the improbable name of Angel whose own dealings ranged from drug dealing and pimping to the occasional 'snuffing out a problem as opposed to sniffing it out!' a quote made mostly (and with much amusement) by himself. A generous trust fund convenient left by a distant aunt had seen Jimmy's passion for Charlie happily taken care of.

A piercing scream followed by sobs of 'No! No! Please no! No more! No more! Stop it! Oh please stop it!' immediately drew Paulo's attention once again to the darkened area of the small cul-de-sac.

'What the fuck?' A curious Paulo made his way cautiously over towards the sounds of what could only be described as someone in acute distress. A final piercing shriek was followed by a few scuffles and a grunted 'Let's get the fuck out of here!' Within seconds a group of shadowy figures emerged from the darkness and, while seemingly adjusting parts of their clothing, made their way quickly back to the brightly lit side entrance to the hotel. Another muffled sob and groan followed their departure.

'Hello? Anybody there?' questioned Paulo foolishly, knowing damn well that there was.

'Oh help me, please help me!' came a voice, muffled with sobs.

Peering into the gloom Paulo noticed a hunched up figure lying alongside a dark Estate Car, the person curled in a foetal position, the hands held protectively towards the groin area.

'Oh my God!' Paulo immediately recognised the sobbing figure as that of the dreaded Titania Delevine, but a very dishevelled Titania, her dress torn and raised above her midriff, displaying a dark, what appeared to be a bloody dripping gash.

'Shit!' said Paulo for want of a better word. 'Oh shit!' he said again. Leaning forward he whispered to the trembling, whimpering girl who was now watching him with terrified eyes. 'Shhhh! Titania! You're safe now,' he whispered soothingly. 'I'm a friend. Here, let me cover you up and then put on my jacket. I'll then have to leave you for a moment and go and get some help.'

'Noooo!' The wail came out in almost a shriek. 'No! No help! I don't want people to know! Please, please! Can't you take me home?'

Paulo looked down at the grief stricken creature, a look of genuine concern on his ghoulish face. 'Are you sure? If you don't want any help can I at least take you somewhere so you can tidy yourself up a bit? If I take you home in your present state your parents will insist on calling the police.' He paused for a moment before adding rapidly. 'They'll see you've been badly assaulted (Paulo couldn't bring himself to use the term 'raped!').

As Titania gave out another despairing moan Paulo suddenly found himself taking on a new, glowing persona; not only was he Paulo the perfect but now it was time to become Paulo, the knight in shining armour!

'Look Titania, let me help you along to my car. I have a friend who has a flat nearby. We can go there and you can get yourself together. Then I can take you home and no one will be any the wiser.'

Titania looked up at the dimly lit face peering so solicitously down into hers. No, Titania didn't see the grotesque, daily parody of the dreaded Paulo Roderiguez! Instead she saw a Mills and Boone hero and promptly fell in love. Paulo in turn, looking down at the shivering girl now cradled in his arms, didn't see the brittle, much maligned Titania Delevine! Instead he saw a fair damsel in distress and himself as the strong hero about to save her. Now it was his turn to fall into the same glorious, heady, earth-moving emotion.

'What the fuck's she doing here and Christ, what happened to the bitch!'

'Shut your face, Rock and get in the back. Titania's been hurt, you twit and I'm taking her somewhere she can get herself together and tidied up before taking her home.'

'And where's that, if I may ask? She looks as if she'd be better off in the nearby A & E – or else a skip!'

Paulo wheeled round, glaring at the petulant, sulking young man. 'One more fucking word out of you and you can walk back to your bloody house!'

A low groan from the front passenger seat where Titania had now collapsed, prevented anymore conversation. Giving Rock another glare Paulo punched in a number on his mobile. After a few seconds it was answered. 'Jimmy, Paulo. I have a person here with me who has had an accident and I need to bring her to your place so that she can tidy up before I take her home. Yes Jim, a her and you know her by sight. Titania Delvine.' The tirade from the earpiece was audible throughout the car. 'Jim! Jim! She's hurt and I'm bringing her round to the flat. Now! We've nowhere else to go. We'll be there in about ten minutes.' Paulo clicked the phone off and turned on the ignition.

'Who's this Jimmy, then?' The question came petulantly from the back of the car.

'A friend,' snapped Paulo curtly, leaving it at that but meanwhile holding Titania's hand which was clutching his gratefully in return.

To Paulo's relief Jimmy could not have been more helpful. A composed Titania – she had spent at least half an hour in the bathroom before emerging looking clear eyed and calm, her dress more-or-less reassembled – had joined the three back in the small, cluttered sitting room of Jimmy's cluttered basement flat in Bina Gardens near to South Kensington.

While Titania was out of the room Paulo had described in hushed tones as to what he believed had happened. Doug Williams and his cronies had simply decided to have some crude fun at the unpopular Titantia's expense. 'So they decided on a gang bang,' said Jimmy, summing up the situation. He gave a small snigger. 'Well, at least the poor bitch won't go to her grave complaining she's never been fucked!'

'That's a shitty thing to say!' cried Paulo (an unfortunate response considering Jimmy's predilections!). 'That "poor bitch" could have been killed for all you care!'

'Whoa! Paulo! Whoah!' Jimmy raised his hands in mock supplication. 'I was only teasing…'

'Well, don't!' sniped Paulo with an intensity which startled both the swimming ace and Rock.

Meanwhile Rock's mind was racing. Who is this guy? He was thinking, and how is it that Paulo knows him? They seem like old friends and yet I've never heard him mentioned. A twinge of jealously tweaked his mind. Yes, old and almost intimate friends...

A testy Rock insisted on being dropped off at Sloane Square from where he would catch the night bus back to his home thus leaving Paulo free to drop off Titania in nearby Chester Square. 'I'll call you tomorrow!' he had hissed into the driver's window but, to his irritation, noted that Paulo seemed more interested in Titania's welfare than his own.

A softly smiling Titania had given the young man a light kiss on the cheek before saying softly. 'Thank you again, my hero!' to which Paulo's only blurted response had been 'See you at college on Monday but hey, if you're up to it and free for supper tomorrow, let's go out?'

A starry-eyed Titania softly agreed.

'*The* Titania Delevine? You mean the daughter of the MP? The one whose mother makes Ivana Trump look as if she's about to take up selling The Big Issue? My Paulo is taking this girl out to supper?'

'Yes, Ma. Tonight. To her favourite place, an Italian restaurant called Manicomio which is near to their house in Chester Square.'

'Chester Square? Isn't that where the old ex-Prime Minister also lives. That Mrs Thatcher?'

'Yes, Ma!'

'Oh, Paulo. Your mother is so proud of her beautiful son!'

Christ, thought Paulo smiling inwardly. Next she'll be calling the bans at the local paedophile palace (his term for the local Catholic church). Smiling openly at his rapturous mother he added. 'Maybe next time I'll ask her back here,' before adding wickedly. 'Roses are her favourite flower!'

'And I'm sure this lovely girl must look like one!' said Mrs Roderiguez not to be outdone by her son's obvious infatuation.

Paulo, whose only sexual experiences had been with Rock and Jimmy found himself in bed with Titania a week later. Titania, more traumatised by her rape than she had let on, refused adamantly her returning to college. Mrs Delevine, being a shrewd but considerate woman had not pursued the sudden decision – she was well aware that something sudden and shattering must have happened to influence her daughter's change of heart but decided – as she had said to her husband – to 'let sleeping dogs lie.' Titania, after a few days of seemingly drifting had surprised her parents even more by saying that she wanted to 'help mother in her businesses.' and became an eager trainee in one of Mrs Delevine's chain of real estate offices. The change in her daughter however, seemed one for the better and when, on asking the young woman if there was, by any chance 'someone now in her life' she had been stunned to receive the most beatific smile in reply. A smile which more than answered her question!

Paulo was enchanted with their new relationship, while Titania ecstatic and Rock simply furious. Almost overnight his lover had appeared to have genuinely turned into a suave, smooth Lothario whose once completely dishonourable intentions were now alarmingly honourable and with a young woman, to boot! A chance meeting with Jimmy 'the port in the storm' the night of the rape had led to a cup of coffee and onto a club which, to Rock's surprise, turned out to be more gay than straight. To his chagrin he had been deserted by Jimmy halfway through the evening and had made his own way home alone. Despite Jimmy's promises to 'keep in touch,' Rock doubted as to whether they would ever meet up again. Two days later Jimmy called.

Meanwhile, the promised dinner had taken place and an over-excited Mrs Roderiguez – a top class cook herself – had pulled out all stops and hired a special caterer for the evening. If the startling appearance of her son's 'princess' had come as a surprise his mother, with true filial devotion, had overlooked the girl's unfortunate faults with the resigned attitude used by millions of mothers through the ages, 'As long as he's happy.'

Titania, to give her her due, had behaved impeccably, praising the decor of the house (she later confided to her mother it epitomised the term Jewey Louis!) and the never ending vases of roses (Titania loathed roses) which the giggling girl revealed to her bemused parents were even to be found in abundance in 'two vases in the guest loo!' Her moment of complete acceptance into the family fold was on inviting Paulo and his parents to join her and her parents for a gala charity event being held at Covent Garden. Two added attractions – firstly, a royal (although somewhat minor) being present and secondly, the Delevines having taken a private box for the occasion, saw the excitement of Rita Roderiguez surpassing even that of winning her first gold at the Chelsea Flower Show.

It had only been on Titania's almost hysterical insistence that the invitation had been reluctantly offered. Both Hugo and Diana, subjected to a hysterical declamation about 'the man I love' thought it better to acquiesce than argue. After all, Titania and never had a boyfriend never mind a man before. Their reactions on meeting the winner of their daughter's affections had been one of immediate disappointment (Hugo, in the privacy of their elegant bedroom suite had referred to Paulo as a 'smarmy spic prick' to which his wife had whole heartily agreed) followed by one of resignation and, if they had been quite honest with each other, relief.

It had not taken much time after the over-elaborate and over-long dinner had ended before Paulo offered to show his princess the summer house. Minutes later Titania, another Charles Svingholm number (this time a dream of silvery satin) was again being subjected to – this time – welcome, frenzied sexual coupling as opposed to the former rape.

In his drama 'The Mourning Bride,' William Congreve, the seventeenth century dramatist has his heroine Zara saying the immortal words, 'Heaven has no rage to hatred turned, nor Hell a fury like a woman scorned.' In his own personal drama as the mourning figure, Rock saw himself as the scorned substitute for the insanely jealous Zara. Bitter and literally ill at his lover's betrayal Rock's every waking moment was built around revenge.

His hatred for both Paulo and Titania was rapidly becoming an all embracing sickness and even his new romance with the sadistic, perverted Jimmy did nothing to appease him. Jimmy, to his own amazement had found himself besotted by the difficult young man. Every perversion possible between two humans had been permitted by the insatiable Rock – in between his bouts of darkest depression – and for once Jimmy had been able to indulge his wildest fantasies with abandon.

Well aware that the wretched Paulo was the cause of his lover's malaise Jimmy was determined to put an end for once and for all – to the cancer eating away at his disturbed but sublime lover's mind. Matters came to a head when, after one particular energetic bout of fisting, water sports and the inevitable scatting, that Jimmy insisted that the problem be resolved and never 'referred to again.' Jimmy even went so far as to say that he was prepared to enter into a civil partnership with the young man if Rock would have him!

Rock expressed his wildest desire.

After a long, silence Jimmy looked at his tearful lover, his shit-smeared face now proud possessor of two rivulets of glistening tears. 'OK, I'll have it sorted out for you, my darling. Have no fear, your devoted Jimmy has his very own guardian Angel for his other angel!' Without hesitation he lifted his mobile punched in the number of his West Indian drug dealer accomplice.

Five weeks later one of the biggest scandals of the decade was to shatter the quiet, complacent elegant suburb of Wimbledon. Two young people – rumour had it they were about to announce their engagement – had been found murdered in what appeared to be some bizarre ritual killing. Paulo Roderiguez (according to the press) a handsome, popular twenty two old and his fiancé-to-be (again, according to the press) the beautiful Titania Delevine, twenty year old daughter of the popular Member of Parliament, had been found stabbed to death in the summer house of the Roderiguez family mansion. Both had been subjected to a vicious rape and both had been killed by a wooden stake, two of the many supporting the bereaved mother's favourite blooms which grew prolifically around the scene of the crime.

On hearing the news a giggling Rock could not help himself from saying to the adoring Jimmy, 'His mother, the overweight old bitch always said her son was the ultimate stake in her heart!'

Later, the giggling young man, lay sprawled on his back, his face turned upwards, his eyes looking hungrily at his squatting lover's muscular buttocks clenched tightly together above him. 'Well done Angel and thank you, darling Jimmy, again and again, is all I can say!' he repeated for the umpteenth time.

His only response from a frowning Jimmy was the curt command. 'Stop talking, cunt face, and open wide!' followed by a grunt and the additional comment, 'Besides, it's rude to talk with your mouth full!' as his first powerful bowel movement began.

FISHERMAN'S PIE

Big Angus looked over at the young man perched on a small stool a few metres away from him, his fishing rod held firmly in his strong, brown hands and reaching out from between his slim, muscled suntanned thighs like a long, thin teasing phallus. The big, bluff, ruddy-faced middle-aged man gave an inward groan at the sight, his mind doing cartwheels at the thought of the young man's proper rod – a rod and no doubt a staff which bring anyone – lucky enough – the most enormous amount of satisfying comfort.

All that Big Angus had been able to glean about the youth was he'd introduced himself as Tim – obviously short for Timothy – when buying bait from Dennis's hardware store set just up the High Street. Angus had later been informed by the know-it-all Dennis that Tim and his family had leased the big house overlooking the bay of their small seaside town for the duration of the summer. Tim's father was a writer for television and his mother apparently a celebrated concert pianist, the sound of endless concertos wafting down from the sprawling cliff house being proof to this claim.

On the first day of his appearance on the sea wall Tim had cheerfully acknowledged the solitary figure sitting on a low, small stool, a rucksack alongside him and an old-fashioned style rod in his big, gnarled hands. Big

Angus, giving an embarrassed grunt, had merely nodded in return. The big man's attitude of apparent rudeness was not intentional, the reason behind the curt response being that Big Angus was finally seeing – at long last and in living flesh – the culmination of all his wildest, wettest dreams and passionate longings.

Magazines such as QX and other gay porn tomes posted furtively on a weekly basis (in the obligatory plain brown wrapper!) from his old mate Dickie, now a retired police constable living in a dismal flat in London's equally dismal Earls Court area, could offer nothing as delicious, delectable and as appetising as the vision now standing in front of him.

It was Dickie – an ex lover from their youth – who had, by falsifying the evidence, helped Big Angus escape being charged in an extremely unsavoury incident involving a minor. Angus's failing was an almost insatiable penchant for S and M and an almost catatonic delight in inflicting pain and then buggering his victim through the interminable night.

Taking the older man's curt rebuttal as a sign that he did not wish to strike up any sort of friendly repartee, young Tim had simply given a shrug and, to Big Angus's combination of horror and delight, stripped off his T shirt and shucked off his jeans. Clad only in the briefest of Speedos and a pair of loafers the young man had then earnestly set about putting together his light, aluminium road and eventually baiting the hook. During the whole operation Big Angus's head had remained as if concentrating on his own rod and his rod only while casting furtive glances towards the relaxed young man now perched on the small stool he had brought along with him.

It was on the third day that Big Angus made his move. 'You're not having much luck from what I've been noticing,' he called cheerily.

Tim, staring blankly at the softly moving water ahead of him, gave a start before realising that the words had been spoken by 'the surly old bugger' a few metres away from him. 'No,' said Tim with a stiff smile. 'Unlike you, sir! You never seem to stop pulling them in!'

'It's where you're sat at,' explained Angus. 'There's a drainage pipe from the mainland close by to where you are. The muck coming into the sea there, plus the difference in temperature, keeps the fish away.' He gave a deep chuckle. 'Now, if you move closer to where I am squatting, you'll find your luck changing.' Angus made a beckoning gesture with a broad, beefy, hirsute arm. 'Why not bring your clobber over and perch yourself about there. I promise you we won't get in each other's way!'

'You're on!' said Tim. Gathering up the stool and his haversack he moved over to the spot pointed out. He gave Angus a dazzling smile. 'I'd already told myself that if I had no luck today I'd call it a day!' The young man gave a laugh. 'But now, perhaps with your advice it'll be my lucky day.'

Or mine, thought Angus, his heart lurching.

With the first hour Tim had pulled four splendid fish from the sea. 'Angus (they had introduced themselves within minutes of their introductory conversation), you have the magic touch. This is bloody marvellous!' Smiling excitedly at the beaming man he added, 'Pity we have a rather formidable cook up the house otherwise I'd take this back and suggest we have them for supper.' The young man gave a sudden laugh at the absurdity of his comment. 'Did I say supper? I must be joking. Mum and Dad insist on a formal dinner each night at nine. As we're here on holiday, me being allowed to appear in a shirt and jeans is considered a major bonus! In London it's always a jacket and tie.'

It was then Angus took the plunge. 'Would you like to bring your fish up to mine some evening? I'm quite the local Jamie Oliver in the kitchen!'

'Gosh, Angus. That'd be great.' A slight frown crossed Tim's lightly tanned face, his blue eyes darkening. 'It can't be today or tomorrow – Mum's got some people down from London and so Dad and I will be on parade, but, hey! What about Friday? Friday would be cool!'

'Friday it is then, Tim,' smiled Angus, his heart beating wildly. 'And I tell you what young Tim, if I take today's catch and whatever we get tomorrow, I'll make you the best fish pie you'll ever have tasted!' He gave an excited laugh. 'Even that young Jamie Oliver would be jealous!'

'If your fish pie is as good as your fishing tips, I don't doubt it for a minute!' laughed Tim.

'And Tim,' added Angus, somewhat conspiratorially, 'I'd keep supper at my place under your hat if you don't mind?'

'No, of course not, Angus but,' and here the youth looked slightly confused. 'May I ask why?'

'It's no big secret,' laughed the big man, making light of it. 'It's simply that I enjoy being a recluse and should it get round the town that I've taken to entertaining, there'll be no end to it! We have three widows in Chitting and once they get wind that it could be open house at Big A's, I'll be chased no end!'

'I'm not surprised Angus.' Tim gave a lewd laugh. 'No doubt they all see you as a very fine figure of a man. In fact, the catch…catch, geddit? The catch of the town!'

Tim, being gay and having witnessed endless bears on the busy London club scene had quickly surmised Angus's interest in him. In fact, if Tim was to be truthful with himself, he was rather enjoying the mild flirtation and although he would have denied it most vehemently, Tim was rather enjoying his role of cock teaser.

'Well,' said Angus looking decidedly uncomfortable. 'Let's say that this is one catch that slipped the net.'

'Don't worry, Angus!' Laughed Tim. 'My lips are sealed. In fact,' he added, 'it's perfect. The parents are out for dinner with some friends who have a stately somewhere nearby. This lucky soul, I'm glad to say, has not been invited. I'll simply tell cook that I've decided to eat in the local in the town or better still, say I'll be at the cinema. They're showing A Single Man and, as I have already seen it, if there are any questions I'll have the answers.'

On mentioning the popular gay movie based on the novel by Christopher Isherwood, Tim had given the older man a quick, surreptitious glance. To his chagrin Angus appeared nonplussed by the reference.

Maybe it is only fish pie and I won't be chased round the table after all! Thought Tim with some amusement.

So, if asked, the lad says he's probably going to the cinema, it couldn't be better. Thought Angus.

Friday saw Tim arriving at their usual fishing spot only to find that Angus – who had always been the early bird ('Along with the worms!' as he would tirelessly repeat to a thinly smiling Tim. After all, how long can one go on repeating such an obvious and corny line?) – was not already set up and seated in his usual place.

Obviously this is going to be some fisherman's pie! thought Tim as he deftly assembled his rod. Tim, if he was to be honest with himself, was now regretting having accepted the supper invitation. In fact, he was quite dreading it. 'Christ, the sad old queen will probably get pissed and maudlin or simply boringly pissed, and even worse, come on to me. Christ!' he muttered as he prepared to cast his line. He gave a giggle. 'Well, Big Angus – and I wonder how big that part of you is? – you'll soon find out that this little fish is not for frying!'

Tim had already made up his mind that he would arrive along with a bottle of wine, eat the pie and simply leave. 'The way the old bugger's gone on about the pie it's almost become deified!' he added out loud to a nearby seagull eyeing him balefully.

In the small kitchen of his neat, isolated cottage set a mile and a half out of the town and nestling in a small wood, Big Angus was busily preparing his special fisherman's pie. He checked the potatoes for the mash topping boiling away before turning away to another pot where he had poured in some milk. Seeing the milk beginning to simmer he sprinkled in a portion of saffron. then gave the liquid a gentle stir. Keeping the mixture on a low simmer Angus then added flaked cod (courtesy of Tim) along with mussels, prawns and scallops (courtesy of the local fishmonger). Further preparations included lightly sautéing a leek in some butter, removing the sautéed vegetable, then adding flour to the liquid to form a roux.

'Delicious,' he murmured. 'And now, young Tim, those very extra special ingredients which will see you well and truly hooked!'

Tim dutifully arrived, as requested, at six thirty. 'I've brought along a bottle of Sancerre – I hope you like it?" he said, giving Angus a nervous smile.

'Sancerre? It's my favourite!' smiled the big man genially. 'Come in, come in! Make yourself at home.' He gave the blond young man an appraising look over. 'You look like that singer, Will Young, in that smart blazer of yours! But why not take it off and make yourself comfortable.'

'I'm fine,' said Tim, somewhat self-consciously. 'Maybe later.' He looked round the small, cosy sitting room. Christ, more Miss Marple than Macho Man! Antimacassars, doilies and fringed lampshades? Shit! No wonder the old queen won't entertain! Which then brought back the sobering thought. Then what am I doing here?

'We'll have the wine with our supper,' said the big man jovially. 'Meanwhile, why not some of Big A's special rum punch to start with?'

'Er…fine, Angus. But only a little please. Remember, I'm meant to be at the cinema and it would never do if I came staggering home pissed!'

'But I thought your parents were out to dinner?'

'They were meant to be but then there was a last minute cancellation. Lady Melton, their hostess, has got a flu bug or something like that.'

'Oh,' said Big Angus, his bonhomie momentarily halted. 'Oh. Well then we'd better keep you sober, hadn't we?' After a few strained minutes of small talk Tim gave a sigh of relief when his host – having excused himself and made his way to the small rear kitchen for what must have been the sixth or seventh time – announced in an affected voice, 'Dinner is served, m'lord!'

Sitting himself down at the small kitchen table the young man looked around the cluttered kitchen with barely concealed amusement. The more he judged the cottage along with its owner, the more incongruous the two seemed to be. He's bloody Gulliver in Lilliput Cottage as opposed to Land, he laughed inwardly. Tim looked down in some trepidation at the carefully arranged mound of steaming fish pie heaped on his plate.

'Do start,' smiled his host pouring the wine into a pewter goblet. 'Don't let it get cold.' With that Angus gave a genial smile and raised his own goblet. 'To us?'

To us? Tim gave a start before mumbling a 'Cheers' instead. Christ, he thought wryly, perhaps the old boy really is expecting me to sing for my supper after all! He took another long sip before picking up his fork and attacking his vast heap of pie. It was then that he experienced the first of what was to become an increasing series of dizzy spells.

Fuck! What the hell was mixed into that rum punch? he thought, I've only had two glasses, better go slow on the vino and get some of this damn pie down me. To give the leering old queen his due, it does smell delicious!

Tim took a forkful of pie, selecting a succulent prawn which he swallowed down with a chaser of the wine. Just then another dizzy spell hit him followed by a searing pain in his stomach. Blinking furiously – he certainly wasn't going to allow the older man to see his distress – Tim took another mouthful of prawn and cod mix and again another swallow of the wine. His vision momentarily clear he was able to give Angus a steady, if somewhat, weak smile. 'It really is delicious, Angus. Quite the chef, aren't you?'

Big Angus, who was now staring the youth, a look of pure maniacal lust on his face, said nothing.

'Jesus!' screamed Tim, falling forward onto the table and clutching his stomach. 'Christ!' he screamed again. 'What the fuck have you done to me?' Writhing in agony and screaming even more hysterically Tim fell to the floor. 'Help me! Help me!' he screamed as a searing, burning, tearing sensation ripped through his entrails.

Unmoved and not moving, Big Angus sat watching the young man screaming in agony for what, to Tim, must have seemed an eternity as he rolled about the floor before ending doubled up, clutching his stomach and beginning to copiously vomit up blood. It was then that the big man stood up, slowly unbuckling his belt and unzipping his trousers. Stepping out of these Angus kicked them aside and, bending down he lifted the now semi-conscious moaning Tim onto the kitchen table, sweeping aside the crockery, cutlery and remains of the fish pie onto the floor. Ripping down his victim's trousers and underpants the big man proceeded to viciously bugger the young man, a procedure that was repeated throughout the night.

It was at dawn break that a weary but satiated Angus returned to the cottage. Still in a state of euphoria he began to tidy the kitchen. Taking the remnants of the pie he carefully removed the remaining prawns and from these removed the fish hooks which he had hidden inside them earlier.

'Poor Tim,' he muttered with a smile. 'Well and truly hooked, weren't you lad? But what a catch!' Here the big man couldn't resist adding. 'Jamie Oliver indeed! Does Jamie start off by giving his guests a glass of punch laced with Rohypnol followed by fish pie containing fish hooks? I think not!'

Pouring himself a large brandy Big Angus and sitting back down on the floral patterned, chintz covered sofa in the small sitting room, he stroked his now thick, flaccid crotch appreciatively. 'Well, you've been taken care of for a month or two, my faithful old rod and staff, and didn't our Tim look ever so tortured as he died? One of our most successful to date.' He gave his crotch another pat before giving out a small laugh. 'And didn't old Dan Truscott's pigs look pleased with their unexpected, early breakfast?'

HERONS IN HYDE PARK

She appeared, regularly as the chimes of Big Ben, her once tall, elegant figure now slightly stooped but her step still firm, her head held proudly. David gave her a friendly nod as they passed on the neatly raked, gravel path and, as usual the nod was left unacknowledged. Staring stonily ahead the woman approached the small ringed knoll of grass alongside the busy road and stood silently, the large, wicker shopping bag held slackly by her side. David, having stopped a few yards back, stood watching and waiting for the often-seen before performance to commence. After two minutes – David had timed her before – the woman reached into the bag and, taking a handful of what he could only imagine to be a special mix – she cast the first of many onto the grassy space.

Almost as if choreographed and in perfect synchronisation a pair of Grey Herons fluttered onto the undulating grassy mound and began pecking hungrily at the offerings. The young man, having been told that this particular type of bird was more a loner than of a gregarious nature, had been intrigued by the civilised give-and-take of these two. It appeared almost as if one was saying to the other – 'No, please, after you!' and 'No, please, after you!' Pleasantries taken care of the pair of birds then continued to feast greedily. David checked his watch again, three minutes to go. Exactly on the estimated time more herons arrived and by the end of his usual viewing time – he allowed himself ten minutes – the former, plain grassy knoll was a heaving mass of guzzling birds but without one hint of any aggressiveness among them.

'Incredible,' muttered David to himself. 'I've now seen her do this for over a month. She's always here when I happen to walk through the Park.' He turned away, pondering bemusedly. I wonder if she comes here during the winter and whether she and her gourmet guests put their clocks back like we mere, near normal mortals do?

About to continue his walk home along the side of the inner road which bordered the wide swathe of playing fields and the Serpentine lake set inside the vast green acres of London's Hyde Park, David paused. Looking again at his watch, he muttered. 'No time like the present! I'm not meeting Tony until eight so let's wait and see where our bird lady roosts herself. It must be nearby.' He looked back at where the herons were still busily feeding and at the lone, figure now in frozen silhouette against the soft evening twilight. Almost as if reading his thoughts the woman turned and began to make her way slowly back along the gravel path towards the gates leading through to Knightsbridge and Lowndes Square. Keeping a good twenty paces behind David began to follow. Having crossed the busy road the woman walked briskly into the square proper making her way down towards the end. Half way along she stopped by one of the iron gates leading into the private garden and, taking out a key from the pocket of her coat, let herself in.

David remained walking purposefully, his eyes straight ahead but, on drawing parallel with the gate, glanced to his right. To his surprise he saw the woman leaning over a figure seated in a wheelchair. Even from this distance and from the fact that he didn't slow his pace, David could see the calmness and compassion in the woman's face as she spoke softly to the seated shadow. Completely intrigued the young man circumnavigated the large square making his way back towards the tall, luxurious hotel set at the far end. To his consternation the woman, now pushing the wheel chair, was making her way through a similar gate to the one she had originally entered but on the opposite side. Knowing it unavoidable not to acknowledge the two, David smiled and muttered a weak 'Lovely evening.'

The woman gave him a piercing look. 'It is,' she answered curtly. 'Quite lovely.' Nodding with what could only be interpreted as a dismissal, she checked the road to her left before pushing the chair forward.

'Here, let me help you down over that kerb and I'll see you across and over to the other side.'

'That's very kind,' said the woman with a frosty smile. 'But Peter and I do this daily.' With that she expertly dipped the wheelchair forward, wheeling it sharply across the narrow street and up onto the opposite pavement. Within seconds the small procession had disappeared into the doorway of a luxury block of flats, the door having been smartly opened by a uniformed doorman.

'Bully for you and Peter,' sniped David, 'And so much for chivalry!' He glanced back down at his watch. 'Shit! I'm going to be late. Better get the tube from Knightsbridge and hop off at Earls Court. I only hope the Tone waits and doesn't get the hump and pisses off!'

'Mr David?'

David spun round to see the doorman standing with a tentative smile on his cheery, round face. 'It's Hawkins, sir! From Arlington Street?' The deep voice had now taken on a note of uncertainty.

'Hawkins? But of course! Yes, it is me, young David that was, but now an ancient thirty year old!'

'You haven't changed a bit, sir, otherwise I wouldn't have recognised you, would I, sir?' Hawkins gave a friendly chuckle. 'Hear you're quite a big wheel in the publishing world now, sir. Editor of some posh mag in that Hanover Square, Mayfair.' The old man gave a self-deprecating laugh. 'You can't say I don't keep up on the latest news about my former employees!' He gave another chuckle. 'And how the parents, sir? Last I heard they were living it up in the South of France.'

'Indeed they are, Hawkins. They have a villa near Cap d'Antibes.'

'Give them my regards, please sir, when next you speak.'

'Thank you, I will indeed. And Hawkins, I take it you're now in control here? A very splendid uniform if I may say so.'

'Thank you sir.' Hawkins gave a conspiratorial wink. 'The residents love it, sir. Makes them think them excessive service charges worthwhile!'

David gave a laugh. 'The woman with the young man in the wheelchair? I take it they have a flat here?'

'Ah, yes. Mrs Winston and young Mr Winston.' Hawkins lowered his voice reverently. 'Poor lad, terrible what happened to him. Absolutely terrible.'

'Some sort of accident?'

'Worse than that, sir. Attacked! Beaten up by some thugs. A whole gang of them.' Hawkins gave a furtive look over his shoulder as if afraid of being overheard. He looked up at the handsome young man as if deliberating whether to continue or not but, deciding this particular titbit was too good not to be shared, whispered even more furtively. 'A gay bashing, sir! Young Mr Winston's one of 'em gays!' For a moment it looked as if Hawkins was about to add something along the lines of 'Serve the bugger right!' but thought better of it.

Why, you bigoted old shit! was David's immediate reaction, but he said instead. 'Beaten up? But that's a dreadful thing to happen to anyone, Hawkins. Gay or otherwise.' He gave the man a searching look. Obviously Hawkins had no idea that the young man in front of him was 'one of 'em' otherwise he would not have been so forthcoming. 'Where and when?'

'It get's worse, sir!' said Hawkins, relishing his sudden role as the purveyor of some highly unpalatable news. 'The young lad was beaten up' – here the pause was almost laughably theatrical – 'in a cemetery, sir! That one in Fulham where all them perverts go to get their filthy rocks off!'

Knowing full well that the now garrulous Hawkins was referring to the Brompton Cemetery in Old Brompton Road, a notorious venue for gay cruising, David continued playing dumb. 'Oh?'

'Yes, sir. Young Mr Peter – or so I'm told and I'm not one to gossip sir – must have been visiting one of 'em clubs they have near there. Furthermore, obviously a bit worse for wear having had a drink or two too many, the lad wandered in there and that's where it must have happened. He was found later by some other gays – no doubt themselves up to no good! Mr Peter was in that Chelsea and Westminster 'ospital for several weeks. His nurse tells me 'e's in one of 'em catatonic states. Won't speak; won't try and move; just sits. 'Is poor mother – she's a widder, Mr Winston 'aving passed on some years ago – is a fine lady even she is if a bit uppity! 'As them funny mood swings too, 'erself. Up one day, down the next. But then one can't blame her; a widder with a gay son and one that's also 'ad the shit kicked out of 'im.'

'I must go!' Said David, seething. Yes, I must go before I punch you in your smug, ignorant face you evil old bastard. Shits like you are the ones who should be beaten up!

'I'll give your regards to my parents.' He added before turning abruptly away and making his way to Sloane Street and the underground station at Knightsbridge.

Due to the shortness of the journey via the Piccadilly Line to Earls Court, David barely had time to cool off. Fucking arsehole! He kept thinking. Fucking, ignorant, unfeeling arsehole! It was just as the train drew into the station that another thought flashed through his mind. But why am I wasting my energy on that old twerp, what about that poor woman's son?

'Penny for them?' Tony, a skinny, bleached blond and a student at a local school of interior design, sat eyeing his friend quizzically across the table. The two had met up at a favourite haunt of Tony's, the popular Balans restaurant, a well known Earls Court gay eatery situated in the Old Brompton Road.

'Certainly worth more than a penny,' came the cryptic reply.

'Well, excuse *moi*!' camped Tony, his eyelashes fluttering. 'First, she keeps this lady waiting and now she's in a snit, to boot! *Mon dieux!*'

'Oh, for Christ's sake, Tony! Cut the camp crap! You can't speak fucking French! You never will and yes, I am in a snit, as you so put it!' He gave the wide-eyed young man an exasperated sigh. 'Not that you would understand...'

'Well, try me!' said Tony pursing his lips and putting his long, slender fingers together, 'Tell Sister Tonette! As they say, a problem shared is not as much fun as sharing a bed!'

'Oh, fuck off, Tone. Here.' David pulled a twenty pound note from his wallet. 'This should cover my wine and your Margarita.' David, now standing, looked down at the bleached, smirking young man, his stomach physically churning. He pulled another note from his wallet. 'And put that towards a better dye job. You need it!'

Apart from a few titters from a couple at the table adjacent to theirs, there was silence from the stunned Tony. Giving his date a final glare David then marched out. 'Stupid queen,' he muttered as he made his way down the Brompton Road back towards Egerton Gardens in South Kensington where he owned a small but comfortable flat bequeathed to him by a doting aunt. Now you Tony, you are certainly one gay who – at times – deserves to be beaten up with all that peroxide shit and camping of yours! One can almost forgive the likes of Hawkins!

Slightly embarrassed by his uncharitable thoughts he never-the-less kept comparing the tough, worldly-wise Tony to the frail, defeated figure he had glimpsed in the wheelchair. Tony would never have allowed himself to be found in such a vulnerable situation. Tony, blessed with a set of doting parents and with unlimited means had drifted through drama school, an art school in Paris and now was 'studying' interior design at a prestigious school set inside the grand precincts of Chelsea Harbour. His next foray into the world of commerce could be anybody's guess. Tony's motto appeared or be 'I am utterly outrageous and long may I continue to be so!' His apparel of a skinny pink and gold lurex T shirt, leather waistcoat, velvet trousers and pointed boots had certainly helped in promoting the mantra.

David's mind flashed back to the brief image of the pale, drawn oval face, a face almost Pre-Raphaelite in its perfection – the pale, long hands gripping the sides of the wheelchair just crying out for tender stroking and soothing. Oh no, thought David with horror. Oh no. Get a grip on yourself, Reynolds. For all his faults Tone isn't that sort of a liability and, let's face it, at the end of the day he is a fabulous fuck!

The following evening a resigned David made his way with slow deliberation towards Hyde Park. Although he waited well beyond the scheduled hour, he, like the milling herons, was to be disappointed by the non-appearance of Mrs Winston.

Instead of making his way through the still busy streets of Knightsbridge and back to his flat – he intended to call in at the Enterprise in Walton Street for a glass or two of wine – David found himself drawn back to the leafy precincts of Lowndes Square. Peering cautiously over the railings his heart soared as he saw the solitary wheelchair with the silent figure. Noticing a movement across the square he could make out the stocky figure of a youngish man making his way over to where Peter Winston sat. David's reaction was without any premeditation and without any regard for the consequences. 'Hello!' He called. 'You coming for Peter?'

The figure, having almost reached the wheelchair, looked around in surprise before locating the owner of the voice. 'Indeed!' came the cheery reply. 'It's time for his supper!' The man bent down to say a few words to the seated figure and then made his way confidently over towards where David was standing.

'Well, this is a surprise.' he said with a warm smile. Approaching the railing he held out a broad, freckled hand, smiling appraisingly at the tall, handsome, dark-haired young man smiling tentatively at him in return. 'Mike O'Shea! I didn't know Peter had any friends round here? Come to say hello, have you? That's nice. I'm about the only other person he ever sees apart from Mrs W. I'm his nurse, by the way.'

'David Reynolds. I'm not er... a friend. More of an acquaintance.'

'Friend, acquaintance, what the heck! It's nice to see a new face. Coming in? Hold on a sec and I'll unlock the gate for you.'

'Thanks.' David looked at the kind, rotund, freckled face, topped by a head of the brightest ginger hair he had ever seen.

Mike, catching his glance gave an infectious laugh. 'That's right. All my friends call me Ginger! Come on in!'

'Mike...er Ginger.' David gave an awkward shrug as he edged his way round the now open gate. 'I don't actually know Peter.'

'That's even better,' replied Mike amiably. 'It'll do him good to meet another soul.'

'Where's Mrs Winston?'

'She's had to go up north for a few weeks hence me being here. I'll be staying until she comes back.'

By now the two had reached the wheelchair. 'Peter, Petey, Pete,' said Mike softly in his light, Irish lilt. 'Say hello to David. He's a new friend.'

Slowly the young man lifted his head of soft brown curls allowing David to look down into a pair of the biggest, most beautiful violet-coloured eyes he had ever seen. The pale, perfectly sculptured lips in an even more perfectly sculpted face trembled for a few almost hallowed moments before a soft, tremulous 'hello' came out.

David glanced up at a stunned Mike who was staring at him incredulously. He looked back down at Peter who was still gazing up at David.

'Hello, Peter,' said David, stretching out his arm and placing his hand lightly on Peter's. 'I'm David.'

'Hello, David,' came the shaky, whispery reply.

'Oh my God!' A still stunned Mike was looking at David, his face glowing. 'David,' he whispered. 'David, what have you done? Petey hasn't spoken for two years!'

David, still transfixed by the face below him, forced himself to meet Mike's eyes. 'I haven't done anything Mike. I only said hello.'

'It's a miracle,' whispered Mike, still in a state of shock. 'A real, goddam miracle.' He looked back at the seated young man, tears now filling his eyes. 'He spoke, David. Peter spoke.'

'Of course I spoke, Mike!' Came the soft voice. 'And don't you think it's time we three went in for tea?'

Three weeks later Mrs Winston returned on a bright, Saturday afternoon to find an empty flat and, much to her amazement, a note from the trustworthy Mike.

'If you get back before we return, Peter and self are at the Serpentine. We'll be back by six. Regards, Mike.'

A curious Daphne Winston – Mike had never taken Peter any further than the Square in all the time he had been looking after her son – could hardly wait for their return. Sitting in her small study idly going through the pile of mail that had been left on her desk awaiting her return, her curiosity was doubly aroused by the sound of cheerful voices in the hallway to the flat. 'What on earth...?' Rising to her feet the woman made her way quickly out of the study and into the now empty hall, the sound of voices having moved to the kitchen.

'Mike?' Daphne Winston strode into the large, modern kitchen to be confronted by three standing figures, all three turning to look at her simultaneously. Clutching her slender throat in alarm her look changed to relief when she recognised a grinning Mike and then to total disbelief at the tall, slim, shyly smiling man looking at her, a hand tentatively outstretched towards her.

'Hello, Mum,' said a soft, gentle voice.

'Peter?' His mother's eyes widened before filling with tears. 'Peter?' She whispered again. 'Oh my darling, is that really you?'

'Yes Mum, it's me. I'm back.' Peter moved forward, taking the now sobbing woman in his thin, lightly tanned arms.

'Thank you, God. Oh thank you God," Daphne Winston kept murmuring in between kissing and hugging her now equally as tearful son.

Having finally gained some self control and in between repeated questions of 'But How?' and 'When' she then noticed the silent figure standing in the shadows behind Mike. 'You!' she finally said. 'The man from the park.'

'The man from the park who's a miracle worker, Mrs W. Here, have this brandy while I tell you all. David, a glass of wine for you and Petey?'

'Petey wine?'

'Now, now, Mrs W. Let Mike O'Shea with the only the slightest touch of the blarney tell you all.'

'How can I ever thank you,' whispered Daphne Winston when Mike had completed his story as to how, on meeting David, Peter had instantly began speaking again and within a few days was taking his first few solo steps. 'He can now outrun me and almost outrun David,' the nurse ended, smiling broadly. 'It'll be the marathon next!'

'How can I ever thank you, dear man?' She asked the now smiling David again.

'You tell her, Petey,' he said.

'By letting me move in with David, Mum,' said the young man, his eyes shining. He nodded towards Mike. 'Mike says I'm now almost one hundred percent OK.' He looked at his stunned mother, 'I'd like to move in straight away – like over this weekend.' Taking a deep breath he looked his mother straight in the eye. 'We're lovers Mum, and have been since the day we met.'

Daphne Winston took a deep breath before looking first at her son and then back to David. A solemn-faced Mike swallowed nervously. 'Well,' said Daphne Winston. 'I don't think it's another brandy I need, Mike. How about cracking open a bottle of champagne?'

A year later to the day he had followed her home, David stood waiting by the grassy mound in Hyde Park. On the minute Daphne Winston, no longer stooped but standing proud and with a serene expression on her face, made her way silently to her son's lover's side.

'Thanks for coming, David,' she whispered. 'I just needed the two of us here alone, together, for what is and will always be our own special, secret ceremony.' She nodded in the direction of the two approaching heron. In unison she and David each took a handful of the food mix from the wicker bag, throwing this gently onto the still vacant patch of green.

'Hello Peter, hello David' she said softly as the two, glorious, long legged, grey, soft-feathered birds landed gently on the grass.

'Hello Petey, lucky David,' smiled the handsome young man eyeing the two birds and giving the elegant, gently smiling woman a kiss on the cheek.

'Thank you for bringing my son back to me.' Said Daphne quietly.

'And thank you for bringing me to your son,' smiled David.

'Hello Mum! Hello lover!' came a laughing voice from behind them. Peter smiled as the startled couple spun around. 'You didn't think for a moment I was going to miss out on the very, very first moment of our anniversary did you? And look, David and Mum!' He pointed to a third heron just flown in to join the feeding couple. 'As the old saying goes. And mother came too!'

Two weeks later David was making his way jauntily towards the small enclosure where the herons still came to feed. Daphne had long since given up on coming along to feed the birds, the ritual having ceased soon after Peter's return to health and his moving into Egerton Gardens with David. To his surprise David saw two Park keepers standing by the knoll, deep in conversation, their green Range Rover parked nearby. David nodded to the men, muttering a polite 'Good evening' but stopped when he noticed two feathered mounds lying on the grass.

'Excuse me,' he said, clearing his throat nervously. 'I may be mistaken but are those herons lying there? Part of the flock that feed here most evenings?

'Well, these two won't be, that's for certain,' said the one Keeper gruffly. 'Bloody vandals,' he added. 'No sir, these two appear to have been poisoned. Luckily for the others but unluckily for these two who must have been early. These two early birds – if you forgive the pun, sir – got the unfortunate early poisoned worm.' He turned to his companion who could not resist letting out a slight snigger. 'Well, we'd better bag these two up then. Sorry to have caused any distress, sir.'

'No, that's alright, thank you,' said David with a tight smile. 'These things happen.' Giving the two men a half-hearted wave he continued on his way. Cutting through the narrow walkway adjacent to the army barracks he felt his pace quickening. No, he thought to himself. Get a hold of yourself, Reynolds. There are no such things coincidences. Now almost running he finally reached Egerton Gardens and the large communal door leading to the flat which he and Peter now called home. Fumbling with his front door key he raced into the bright sitting room breathlessly calling 'Petey? Petey? You OK?'

The complete silence caused David to stop in midstride and stand still, listening. 'Petey?' he called again before making his way into the small but practical kitchen, his anxious face breaking into a smile on seeing a note propped up against a mug on the breakfast bar. He scanned the scrawled writing briefly.

Mum having a bit of a downer so have popped round to cheer her up. Thought we'd all have dinner, OK? Love ya! P.

David's smile changed to a small frown of annoyance. Not another fucking downer, he thought to himself. Come on Daphne, you never stop having bloody downers and expecting Petey to come rushing round to hold your bloody hand. And now it's yet another bloody dinner again for three! Still frowning he moved over to the fridge and took out an already open bottle of wine. Pouring himself a glass he stared down at the note again before crumpling it up angrily and throwing it in a nearby waste bin.

'Fuck!' he said aloud to the empty room.

David's concern was twofold; the cloying hold of Daphne Winston on her son and the fact that Peter, despite his now full recovery, had not done anything about getting himself a job, taking any sort of educational course and in fact seeming to spend most of his time in the company of his clinging mother in his role as a constant 'walker' or escort. In one of their now many escalating arguments it inevitably came back to the fact that Peter, with his substantial allowance, was more dilettante than ambitious. To his acute horror David – on more than one occasion – found himself comparing Peter with Tony. At least the Tone is now working with a bona fide design company and not only loving it, but doing extremely well, he was thinking more and more. If he was to be completely honest with himself, David missed the banter and campery of Tony and his friends. The one and only time he had taken Peter to Balans he had had to control himself when Peter, on looking around at the crowded, animated restaurant, had said with a superior smile. 'Not quite Cipriani or San Lorenzo is it?' And this from a young guy who – three years beforehand – had not only been out clubbing in the area but also cruising in the nearby Brompton Cemetery and almost beaten to death.

'Fuck!' he said out loud for a second time. Lifting the receiver to the wall phone he dialled the Lowndes Square number. 'Daphne, David.' His frown increased as he heard high pitched laughter coming over the line. 'May I speak to Peter please.'

'Of course you may speak to Peter,' came the slightly sarcastic reply, the emphasis being on his more formal use of his lover's name.

'David!'

'Petey, this is the second time this week Daphne's had one of her turns and no, I don't want the three of us to have dinner. I want the two of us to have dinner. Capiche?'

He listened to the growing silence. 'Petey?' he asked, thinking that perhaps Peter had inadvertently cut him off.

'I'm still here and yes, David, I'm staying for dinner. Capiche?' With that Peter slammed the phone down.

'Fuck you, too!' hissed David staring at the silent receiver in his hand. After only a minute's hesitation he dailed an old familiar mobile number. 'Tone? David. You free for a drink later? Balans EC would be great. Nine? See you then.'

David looked across at Tony's once familiar grin. 'So there you have it in a nutshell, Oedipus wrecks!' He took another long swig from his glass of Pinot Grigio (they were on their second bottle). 'I mean, don't get me wrong, I love Daphne dearly but, shit, Tone, she simply won't leave Petey alone.' He looked sorrowfully at his glass. 'And he's just as bad. Never off the phone to her; always out to one of their ghastly "girls" lunches and then it's always, but always this bloody dinner thing. Sometimes I think he should simply move back with mummy and forget about us as a couple!'

'It's really that bad, Dave?'

'Bad, Tone? It's fucking doing my head it. It's affecting my work and I can tell you I'm not a happy bunny!' He took a deep breath. ' Christ, we don't even fuck anymore!'

'Ah, now I see the reason for this impromptu drinks invite! Poor Dave – the non-rave – needs old cast-off Tone so he can get his rocks off!'

'Oh, shut up, you idiot!' David couldn't control his burst of laughter. 'Anyway, let's forget Peter and mummy for this evening. C'mon, drink up. I think maybe another bottle?'

'Why not, maestro? After all, when you're with me you're always in the driving seat!

'And a very comfortable seat if my memory serves me well.'

'Touché,' said Tony, clinking his glass against his ex-lover's. He paused for a moment before adding with a mischievous grin. 'Just as well his name isn't Tony!'

'What on earth do you mean?'

'Peter. Just as well he isn't called Tony, him being such a mother's boy and all that.'

'I don't follow you?'

'That case in the seventies, that Barbara something-or-other, the Bakelite heiress who used to fuck her son and was subsequently murdered by him!'

'I don't quite think Peter fucks his mother, Tone,' said David as light-heartedly as he could. 'They're just very close.' He added, a sudden chill running down his spine as he thought back to the two dead herons in Hyde Park. 'And her name was Baekland, Barbara Daly Baekland and they lived in Cadogan Square.'

'Cadogan or Lowndes Square. Who gives a fuck, if you'll pardon the expression.'

'I think we ought to get that new bottle but now!' David beckoned to the chunky, handsome waiter. 'Daniel, another bottle of the Pinot please!'

David returned to the flat, somewhat the worse for wear, having 'closed' Balans at around two a.m. Their meal finished, the two had joined another group and sat drinking until last orders were called. To his chagrin – but not to his surprise – David found the flat empty and, on checking the answering machine, no messages. 'Well, fuck you and you go fuck your fuck-up of a mother as well,' were his last words before falling into an unsettled sleep.

THREE MONTHS LATER:

Derek Williams paused for breath, leaning forward, his hands on his sweat-covered knees. He grinned up at his equally breathless partner. The two had been jogging for the last half hour through Hyde Park and around the Serpentine, a daily routine which not even the severest weather could deter. Taking a deep gulp of the crisp, autumn evening air he nodded in the direction of a lonely figure silhouetted in the dim light of the passing traffic and lights from the windows to the luxurious hotel opposite. He nodded again towards the solitary man, laconically throwing something to a few, shadowy figures on the small mound of grass in front of him.

'See that guy over there? Feeding the birds? You know who that is don't you? He used to be in Balans a lot a year or two ago.'

'So?' His jogging partner looked across at him expectantly.

'It was in all the papers a few month's ago. His lover was apparently poisoned by his very own mother and then the old bird topped herself.' He gave a malicious grin. 'They were found in bed together. Starkers!'

'A case of poison interruptus!' came the quick riposte. 'C'mon, let's trot past the sad widower and see what he's up to.'

Jogging smoothly side by side they passed David standing eyeing what appeared to be two large birds greedily pecking away in the cold, cropped grass. As they were passing David turned and caught Derek's eye. Derek, in his turn felt his heart give a sudden lurch as he noticed the man's pale, handsome face streaming with uncontrollable tears.

CINDERELLA FELLA –
THE STORY OF A HEEL

Algie gave a petulant frown at the prince's silly gesture. Why give the glass slipper back to that stupid Cinderella? Why not keep it for himself?

He wriggled his huge, six foot three, fleshly twenty stone frame in a futile effort to make himself more comfortable on the sagging, stuffing-depleted couch; a leftover from the former tenant of the small, rancid one bedroom flat in which he, Algie – courtesy of the local council – resided free of charge aided and abetted by a miniscule allowance – courtesy of the tax payer – to cover his everyday needs.

'Silly, silly prince!' Algie sniped again, peering down at the simple illustrated book resting on his bloated, blubbery stomach, reminiscent of some stained waterbed (his overstretched T shirt appearing to have a distinct allergy to the likes of a washing machine!). 'Stupid, stupid man!'

Sticking a large, fleshy, hairless finger into his surprisingly hairy right nostril he found – to his surprise, satisfaction and ensuing delight – a large, moist, golden bogey which he lovingly extricated. Still glaring down at the asinine prince Algie carefully placed the tender globule onto his thick lower lip and with his large wet tongue – chameleon-like – flicked the unexpected gourmet offering into his mouth.

'Yum! Yum! Tum! Tum!' he burbled, savouring the momentary flavour before returning the aforesaid finger to the left nostril where, to his chagrin, like Mother Hubbard's cupboard (deemed by Algie to forever be that 'silly, silly old woman!') the nostril was bare.

Turning the page he peered again at the full size illustration of the captivating, sparkling glass slipper. His breath quickening, Algie fumbled greedily at his already unzipped, much finger-marked fly where, his large chest starting to heave even faster, he clamped his bulbous thumb, thick-set index and forefingers heavily around the small pathetic button mushroom-like mound cowering coyly in between a sparse hiding place of wispy hairs. – the object of his frenzied fumbling being nature's witty but cruel suggestion of a penis.

'Silly, silly prince!' Algie gasped again before subsiding into a further whimpering, shuddering, blubbery, flubbery whinnying snort of 'Shitty, shitty Cinders! Shitty, shitty silly, stupid servant girl!'

Giving another mucus-inspired snort accompanied by an extremely large, irredeemable and very wet fart, the heaving mound of man-boy dribbled a small bubble of translucent cum into his pink, damp, and greedily receptive palm.

'Honestly, Algie!' Dolores Espades gave a theatrical sigh as she continued glaring at the large, whale-like figure humped over the steaming sink. 'You're meant to wash the dishes! Wash them, Algie! Not dip and dunk! Wash, rinse and wipe, Algie! Wash, rinse and wipe!'

The small, dark Latino-looking woman (Dolores was Camberwell born and bred) gave another exaggerated sigh. 'At times I don't think you give two hoots about our customers or our reputation! Casa Mia is an upmarket establishment with a reputation for the best Spanish cooking outside Madrid and not some tacky tapas bar!' She gave a derisive snort before adding her usual mantra repeated endlessly throughout the day. 'Our clients are more Valentino than vulgar!'

Poor Dolores – her mother having named her after Dolores Del Rio the Mexican actress of silent movie fame and later the talkie, Flying Down To Rio – had, before marrying the dashing Miguel Espades, coveted the idea of entering the Rank Charm School and then taking J Arthur and his colleagues by storm before repeating a similar natural phenomena in Hollywood. The charm school had failed to materialise whereas the well-endowed Miguel hadn't. Swept off her diminutive feet by the handsome waiter Dolores found herself rapidly pregnant and, being a bad girl decided to become a good Catholic one instead, thereby marrying her saviour. The mere fact that hubby was Spanish through and through from his greasy black locks down to his impressive pee pee and magnificent cojones (there was no need to glance down any further) and not a chicano (Miguel's observation) Dolores still went on day dreaming of being the new Dolores Del Rio. Two children arrived and left as soon as they were able to fly the family nest while Miguel, to his own and his hardworking wife's surprise, ended up inheriting Casa Mia from the grouchy old owner, a wizened Signora Pasco, who – unbeknown to Dolores – had been regularly sampling Miguel's legendary pee pee and Wimbledon-worthy conjones over the years.

To put it simply, Dolores, through her impulsive marriage had achieved the dubious status of many a woman of aspirations, the accolade of a 'Never Been' as opposed to the somewhat more elevated status of a 'Has Been.' In her eyes, her position as manageress of their shabby, squalid restaurant was more char-person than chairperson.

Miguel however, revelling in his status as proprietor, simply told his long suffering wife to 'get on with eet' and stop complaining. The arrogant, layabout Spaniard's main function in his heady role as owner appeared to be a dedication of almost religious fervour in wearing out as many packs of playing cards as obsessively possible.

While the ever complaining Dolores slaved away either in helping Aldo, the slovenly cook or chivvying along Mavis, the slatternly waitress (to add a touch of Spanish authenticity Mavis wore a bright red plastic Hibiscus flower in her sparse, badly dyed, dull black hair), her husband would be playing cards with his cronies in the small so-called office at the back of the dingy premises. Card playing alternated with the very regular – and frantic – fucking of one, Hermione Barbados, a large, jolly black woman who worked in the local benefits office. It was the Rubens-esque Hermione who had suggested that Dolores take on the child-like Algie 'as a favour.' The mere fact that Algie, unaware of the legal luxury of a minimum wage, had happily accepted a subsidy of one pound an hour plus meals – usually a leftover plate of dubious paella termed crudely by Mavis as Algie's fart fodder – or the occasional sad, soggy Spanish omelette (Aldo's house speciality).

Much to Dolores chagrin, Algie would sometimes attempt to cook in the small kitchenette back at his sordid flat. The woman was always berating the shamed man-child for borrowing cooking utensils and failing to return them (his passion was for the skillet pan) or else absent-mindedly taking the odd potato, cutlet or plastic container of sauce made to the cook's secret recipe, the secret being one which hopefully – or so thought Miguel on numerous occasions – Aldo would take to his grave.

Algie gave a sullen nod before simply dunking – neither wiping nor rinsing – another smeary plate and promptly dropping it. 'Sorry Dolores,' he wailed in his strange, high flute-like whisper, backing away from the small, glaring woman. 'It slid because it's slippery!'

'I'll "slid" you!' shrieked Dolores. 'Merdé' she added viciously. 'That fat cow Hermione has a lot to answer for! (Poor, ignorant Dolores, many a word spoken in jest…). She reached angrily for a mop. 'Now, clean up the broken bits and then go and help Mavis clear those empty front tables which those patrons have just left.' She gave another exaggerated sigh before handing over the mop. 'And do try not to drop anything!'

It had been on Miguel's insistence (via Hermione's insistence) that Algie should get some 'front of house' experience. This request was duly conceded to but only when the small restaurant was either empty or limited to a carefully watched table. Algie's greatest achievement so far had been to remember that one cleared from the right as opposed to the left. An ever vigilant Mavis had drummed this into the shambling man-boy by a series of painful pinches to his large, fleshy right buttock!

On this particular day a solitary figure had been left sitting at a small side table. The figure, a woman, sat sipping thoughtfully on a glass of sangria, a small plate of black olives nestling against a sheaf of papers loosely lying inside a pale blue translucent folder, the papers in question being deliberately ignored.

Stacey Cotton gave a small sigh, crossing her short, stocky legs impatiently, the quicksilver gesture causing her even shorter skirt to rise provocatively up against her even more chunky thighs. A small right foot bounced rhythmically in time to the distinct flamenco beat of Paco De Lucia playing softly on the MP3 player (Dolores's only acknowledgement to modern day technology) with Stacey's right shoe, a sexy, strappy number in bright red faux patent leather with teasing, rapier-like stiletto heel (more phallic than formidable) dangling precariously as it bobbed and bounced on the black nylon encased foot. Her left foot, similarly enhanced and not to be outdone, tapped Astaire-like in unison on the blue ceramic tiled floor.

Algie stopped abruptly in mid-shuffle, his bulbous watery eyes riveted on to the dangling, tantalising siren-of-a-shoe as it jumped, shimmied and shook in the feeble light of the wall sconces and the lone 'atmospheric' candle gamely spluttering on Stacey's table.

For Algie it was lust at first sight.

Forget Cinderella's unrealistic glass slipper! And anyway, how could a mere drawing, even if in colour and even if in a book of fairy tales ever hope to compete with the vision before him; a vision of pure, undiluted, pornographic, almost biblical perversion and perfection? The spiked heel, reminiscent of the largest thorn on Christ's crown; the thin red straps representing the bright red rivulets of the Redeemer's blood. Sagging in almost a state of perverse genuflection, Algie's already slack, prehensile jaw slackened even more as a hiss of halitosis was duly followed by a glistening dribble of saliva making a slow descent over his cherubic, hairless chin before plopping onto his shirt front.

Along with the facial processes Algie's button mushroom also decided to more than simply mushroom. Though not quite atomic cloud in its stature as a mushroom cloud, Algie discovered for the first time in his twenty years, his man-boy's little penis becoming decidedly more projectile than pencil.

'Yes?'

Stacey's snapped, impatient question startled Algie out of his lust-infused trance.

'Oh… I was just checking everything's OK.' Algie's startled response came out in its high, child-like, sibilant whisper, the complete antithesis as to what would have expected from so formidable a frame. This single response to any customer's would-be acknowledgement of the lumbering giant's presence had been patiently drilled, on a daily basis by the ever exasperated Dolores, into Algie's sad, retarded excuse for a memory.

The whispered response was accompanied by a loose, wet, tremulous attempt at a smile.

'Everything's fine, thank you!' snapped Tracey thinking, Christ! What's a fuckin' retard like you doing in a dump like this? Even though it is a shit heap!

The woman couldn't resist a snigger at her crude wit. A slow shit in a shit heap? Tracy gave another snort. Dumped in a dump? Unable to hold back a bout of laughter she quickly reached for her glass and shakingly held it to her heavily painted lips while giving the large child-like edifice a mocking look.

Seeing his large, bulbous egg-like eyes riveted on her still jiggling foot, she hastily stopped the bouncing. 'But you can get me another sangria, now!' she added curtly, the snapped command accompanied by a shudder of revulsion at the now sweat covered, oversized, quivering cherubic face.

Giving – to Stacey's surprise – an equally curt nod, the attempted smile instantly obliterated, the large figure slowly turned away from the woman who, to her horror, was subjected to a silent but lethal fart at face level. Almost gagging and gasping for air an apoplectic Stacey reached blindly into her bag for a handkerchief.

An anxious Dolores greeted him at the service door. 'I told you to help Mavis clear, not speak to the customers!' she hissed. She peered around

Algie's formidable frame. 'What did you say to her? She looks as if she's having some sort of fit?'

Algie gave an undulating shrug. 'She wants another singra, that's all.'

'A sangria, Algie. San-gri-yah, not a sin-gra!' The tiny woman shook her dark head in feigned exasperation. 'And where is Mavis? She's supposed to be in charge of the front of house!' (Dolores expectations of Casa Mia stoically remained at the highest of levels, even when – in the past – mass immigrations from rodents to roaches had proved a threat to their reputation).

'Dunno,' muttered Algie before adding with an almost rapt expression, 'Toilet!'

Dolores gave another shake of her head. 'Can't leave you two alone for a moment, can I?' She glared up again at the large, vacuous face. 'Can!?' she repeated loudly before realising that Algie's interest was obviously elsewhere and in some transcendental faraway place known only to himself.

Algie, in fact, was in an almost catatonic state being simply mesmerised by the vision of the red, dancing shoes and the never-before experience of his usual small, difficult-to-get-hold-of messy mound being now transformed into a bouncing larky lollipop!

'I give up,' muttered Dolores, with an added muttering of, 'Blast you, Hermione Barbados!' Turning on the still zombie-like man-boy she added more loudly. 'You get back into the kitchen and I'll deal with the customer's sangria!'

Two days later the body of Stacey Cotton was discovered by two boys playing truant and about to have a mutual, satisfying wank in their favourite wanking spot, a dense conglomeration of rhododendrons and laburnum bushes growing close to a shortcut across a small heath and nearby to the Red Lion Pub, a mere five minute walk from the Casa Mia and the dilapidated High Street.

From what Dolores and the other locals were able to glean from the evening paper, gossip and a supposedly genuine police statement, there had been no evidence of any assault, sexual or otherwise. Cause of death had been a blow to the head by some heavy blunt instrument which, even after an extensive search among the neighbouring bushes, had not been found.

Robbery was also ruled out as a motive, the woman's handbag being found lying close to the body with purse and money intact. What little jewellery Stacey had been wearing, a wristwatch, bracelet and ring on her pinkie finger, had also remained untouched. The only missing item was the red shoe from her right foot.

That same evening, an eager Algie shuffled home, his increased pace rate a sharp contrast to his usual lethargic, dragged steps. Back inside the haven of his sordid little flat he quickly stripped off his work clothes, throwing them carelessly onto the well-worn carpet. Stark naked, his giant, hairless, bulbous pink form glowing wax-like in the weak glow of a small table lamp, the trembling man-child knelt reverently alongside the saggy, soiled single bed. Feeling eagerly beneath the cold metal frame he slowly withdrew an old shoe box (one of a pair) from its hiding place, a look of total rapture of his large face. His large hands now shaking wildly he grasped the single, red stiletto shoe with his tremulous fingers.

Lifting the shoe to his gaping nostrils he inhaled its aroma deeply before gently licking the shiny, inner sole. His breathing rapidly increasing, he slowly sucked on the thin, gleaming, red spiky heel.

Emitting ecstatic groan after groan he continued sucking, sniffing and licking, his now rampant, newly inflamed penis almost matching the red tone of the delectable shoe.

With a further, more guttural groan he leaned his large head down towards the counterpane but not before spitting volubly on the heel. With a deep throated sigh he positioned the shoe behind his back and then down between the cleft of his large, soft, pillow-like buttocks before viciously impaling the sharp heel inside his already torn, raw, tender and already repeatedly shafted anus.

Several repeat performances later combined with sobbing, dribbling orgasms the satiated mound of the blubber-like Algie fell into a dreamless, innocent sleep on the – by now – blood stained carpet, the instrument of his delight still impaled – this time toe first – inside his rectum.

Several days later a blood splattered skillet was found by a diligent dustman emptying a wheelie bin close to Algie's block of flats. Putting two and two together – Bert, the dustbin man was an avid viewer of 'Crime Watch' and had read about the mysterious murder of Ms Stacey Cotton in the local papers – the suspicious man had immediately contacted the police.

The photograph of the murder weapon, an inoffensive cooking utensil, was later given television coverage in a news flash that same evening. Like the vigilant Bert, Dolores put two and two together but not before a sleepless night. In the cold light of day, Algie or no Algie, she called the police from the reassuring surroundings of Casa Mia. Although she could not – and would not – swear on the Holy Bible that the skillet was hers, she was more than sure it was (Dolores had lost count years ago of her vast, motley array of kitchen utensils).

An hour later the police descended on Algie's flat to find the strange young man already dressed in his de rigueur outfit of loose, baggy trousers with T shirt (a clean one supplied daily by the ever fastidious Dolores) and about to leave for work.

A quick questioning of the man-boy proved more frustrating that fruitful and a quick search of the premises while the suspect stood silently and morosely by, found nothing that could possibly be seen as suspicious. A momentary excitement on the discovery of the shoe boxes was quickly extinguished when Algie pointed to the scuffed pair on his large feet.

It was only later that evening that Mavis, after continually noticing a strange bulge protruding from the seat of Algie's baggy trousers, she and an even more curious Dolores found themselves with no alternative but to pull an irritated Miguel away from his card playing friends to also 'have a look.'

A reluctant but curious Miguel had then been given the embarrassing task of asking Algie as to what was tucked away in his trousers. Had he stolen something from the kitchen, some food or even a bottle of wine? Miguel demanded to know.

Staring sullenly at the floor Algie refused to respond until Miguel, in a flash of latent Spanish fire, clutched at the curious bulge.

'Christ!' had been his only response before ripping down the baggy apparel. 'Mio Christos!' he had gasped again just as Dolores fainted and Mavis screamed.

Sticking proudly from between Algie's spectacular buttocks was a bright red heel with the toe and sole of the shoe nowhere to be seen.

MARY POPPINS IS A CUNT!

'Jesus!' panted Nigel, 'I don't believe it! Now it's starting to bloody well rain!'

'Don't be such a wimp!' panted Rupert, equally as breathless. 'It's only a light drizzle and,' he added, pausing for a moment to take a deep breath of the warm, moist air, 'As that Andie MacScowl says in those dreary, misleading adverts of hers, "I'm worth it!"'

Nigel couldn't resist a warm grin. 'At eight thousand feet above sea level that may take some proving!' He gave a chuckle. 'But don't let it ever be said that Nigel Collins isn't a player.' He took another deep breath. 'He'll see what he can manage back at the ranchero!'

'You're on but let's get on with the present one. Lead on Macduff!'

'As her ladyship commands!' Giving out another chuckle, Nigel began climbing the steep, narrow, well-worn path ahead of them.

Nigel Collins – late thirties, tall, good-looking in an archetypal English way (blond hair, blue eyes, strong chin and a lean build) and his lover, Rupert Landau – mid twenties, slim, dark haired and dewy-eyed (more elfin than elegant) were nearing the end of their long climb up the main peak of the two prominent landmarks which dominate the famous ruined city of Machu Picchu in Peru. The ancient Inca city, the highlight of a holiday in celebration of the fifth anniversary to their Civil Ceremony in

London, was to be the final stage of their 'South American Sexcelebration' as Rupert wittily called it.

'Only a few more yards to go and then we're at the top,' puffed Nigel. 'Not too good for the old ticker,' he murmured to himself, momentarily conscious of a warning from his GP during a routine check up. 'The old blood pressure needs taking care of, Nigel. All work and no play could make our Nigel a very sad boy!' Hence another reason behind the holiday. He paused for a moment, looking at the spectacular vistas surrounding them. Waving at the nearby peaks of the Andes and then pointing down at the tiny, narrow serpent-like silver thread of the Urubamba River way below, he softly added. 'Jesus Rupie, just look at this view. Even though we're seeing it all through a light rain, my God, unlike your Andie MacScowl, this is certainly worth it!' He peered up at his companion ahead who, for some strange reason known only to himself, was now crouching behind a large boulder close to the summit.

Turning with a mischievous grin Rupert beckoned Nigel on and at the same time indicating to him to remain quiet.

'What?' whispered Nigel crouching down beside him and giving the young man's hand an affectionate squeeze.

'Look,' his companion whispered back, stifling a giggle. 'Forget your Incas and their priests... get a load of that!'

Nigel, his eyes following his lover's pointing finger found himself stifling a snort of laughter. The object of their amusement – the 'that' of Rupert's observation – was an athletic young man sitting silently on top of the highest boulder set on the summit of the majestic peak, an umbrella held firmly in one hand and what appeared to be a bottle of champagne, in the other. As the two watched the lone figure sitting in what could only be described as a state of complete, hedonistic bliss, the silhouette took a slow, deliberate sip from the neck of the bottle.

'Now I've seen everything!' chuckled Nigel more loudly than intended. ''Jesus! It's bloody Mary Poppins!'

'I heard that!' said the lone figure turning towards them with a grin from beneath the brolly. 'And no, you're mistaken. It's not bloody Mary Poppins! It's bloody Machu Poppins!'

Several hours later, Nigel, Rupert and their new friend Mike aka Mary Machu Poppins Mayhew were sitting on the small scenic train now returning to Cuzco, the main Andes town (set three thousand feet higher in the mountain chain than the famous, ancient city). Like their new found companion, the two men had taken the day trip to Machu Picchu and were now happily seated together in the bar section of the small, mountain train sipping the first of several pisco sours (a lethal cocktail made from pisco – a fermented grape-like brandy – lime, sugar and blended with egg whites) and generally getting to know each other.

Nigel, to his alarm, found him staring at their new found mountaineer friend with a predatory lust which, since his meeting up with Rupert, had lain decidedly dormant. Christ, what am I thinking? he thought crossly. He smiled guiltily towards his partner. 'Drink OK?' he questioned for want of something to say and thus drawing himself away from Mike's own appraising and deeply penetrating, deep blue eyes.

'Oh yes,' cried Rupert camply. 'Another of these and I'll be anybodys!'

Mike gave a laugh. 'You'd better watch out, Nigel. Young Rupert here is about to go on a *rape-age*!'

'*Rape-age*?' Rupert turned to Mike with a quizzical expression. '*Rape-age*? Surely you mean rampage? To my vast knowledge as a teacher of the Queen's English' – here he could not resist a camp shriek – 'there is no rape-age!'

'Ah, but there is and you've just said it!' laughed Mike, giving an uncomfortable Nigel a conspiratorial grin. 'A combination of the word "rape" and "age" and, if I may say so, young Rupert, you look the perfectly ripe age for a good old *rape-age*!'

'Hold on! Hold on!' said Nigel flushing angrily. But then, embarrassed by his sudden and irrelevant outburst he added a quick 'You're talking to my nearest and dearest here,' in a lame attempt to diffuse the anger he saw rising in Mike's up-until-now cheerful face. 'If anyone around is going to be doing any Rupie raping, it's his dull old Nigel.' He hastily continued along with a conciliatory laugh. He pointed at the empty glasses. 'I think another round of these, don't you?'

Not waiting for a response from the other two – Mike had relaxed back into his original smiling self and Rupert, a slightly befuddled expression on his almost Pre-Raphaelite face, seemed oblivious to the slight tension that had just arisen – Nigel scooped up the glasses and made his way to the far end of the carriage. Standing waiting to be served at the small bar he silently chastised himself.

Jesus, Collins, the guy was only making a joke and, besides – here he couldn't resist a small snigger of self-satisfaction – if there had been the possibility of any raping to be done I have a strong feeling it would have been between mountaineering Mike and me!

Having formally introduced themselves on the top of the famous landmark at Machu Picchu, the three had companionably finished off Mike's bottle of champagne and then made the cautious, slow descent back down the mountain to the ruins of the old Inca city itself. After a light lunch at the very touristy hotel adjacent to the spectacular site they had eschewed the bus journey back down to the tiny station far below and walked down the steep, winding path instead. Mike had mentioned he worked as a personal trainer for 'the rich and obese' in London and seemed deeply interested in Nigel's obvious success as a City high flyer (Nigel had been one of the big bonuses 'named' for the previous year) and less interested in Rupert's devotion to his role as a teacher of English literature at some nondescript college.

'You positively scream personal trainer!' Rupert had camped during lunch. 'Everything beginning with a "p" seems to apply to you.' He had then given Mike what he considered his best, most vampish, sultry look. 'And I bet that doesn't end with your pecs, Mary!' To Mike's chagrin and to Nigel's embarrassment Rupert's nickname for Mike was, as far as the coquettish young man was concerned, to unfortunately stick.

Any remark by a grinning Mike and a sharp rebuke by an uncomfortable Nigel was thwarted by the intrusion of their beaming waiter offering them another bottle of Torrontes white wine.

Yes, and I know what you're thinking, Rupie, Nigel had thought disloyally at the time. If your face and physique is anything to go by, Mike, your cock must also be perfect! A pure, bloody Michelangelo's David but, hopefully, with a more impressive dick than the apology for the one on the famous statue.

Returning with the replenished cocktails he noted – with some relief – that Rupert had dozed off, his dark head leaning against the window, his rosebud lips slightly parted showing his perfect white teeth.

'Thanks.' A smiling Mike leant forward to take the glass from Nigel's hand, his own hand lightly brushing the other man's. 'I have never managed to carry three glasses at a time,' he laughed, 'even though I have a pair of hands each the size of a plate. 'He gave a light, self-deprecating grin. 'I'm too clumsy by half.'

'I'm sure that's not true,' laughed Nigel. 'Being a personal trainer does not allow one to be clumsy! Can't be seen dropping too many of those weights now, can you? Not a positive image in your business!' Oh Christ, he thought on seeing Mike's bemused expression. Talk about being crass and trying to curry favour at the same time.

'Oh, you'd be amazed at what I can pick up if I want to,' smiled Mike. 'I've never failed yet! Cheers!'

Without any prearrangement it seemed natural for the three to meet up later in the bar of their hotel. 'What are you two doing for dinner?' Mike asked as they sat nursing a further set of pisco sours.

'Nothing in particular,' said Nigel. He looked across at Rupert who again seemed slightly the worse for wear – he still hadn't quite recovered from the amount of wine and cocktails quaffed earlier – 'but I thought we'd check out one or two of those restaurants on the main square.' He gave Mike a nervous look. 'Perhaps you'd like to join us…?'

'That'd be terrific!' enthused Mike, breaking into another of his mischievous grins. 'I'm told that there's a great little restaurant right next to the cathedral which serves the very popular local dish, roasted Cuy.'

'Dinner under the stars in glorious Cuzco,' giggled Rupert. 'And right by the cathedral.' Eyeing Mike archly he couldn't resist adding, 'But not quite with the original Virgin Mary you, Miss Machu Mary Poppins!'

Unfazed, Mike simply gave a laugh. 'More likely a set of Hail Marys when you try the Cuy!'

'And what is this key if I may ask?' enquired Rupert loftily. Giving another camp giggle he eyed Mike coquettishly. 'Maybe the key to my heart!'

'Rupie! Enough!' said Nigel sharply. He turned to a now smirking Mike. 'This local dish, this er…Cuy? What is it, Mike?' He gave a small chuckle as if trying to make light yet again of another outburst. 'Some ancient recipe of the Incas handed down through the centuries?'

'Maybe, maybe not,' laughed Mike. 'All I know it's a local dish that everyone swears by.'

'Yes, but what is it?' This from a petulant Rupert back to Mike while scowling at his lover.

'Roast guinea pig.'

'Guinea pig? I'm not going to eat a sweet, harmless fucking little guinea pig!' Rupert shrieked, his remark causing the heads of several fellow drinkers to turn in their direction.

'Well, you can always try something else,' said Mike hastily. 'Although it's a Mexican dish the restaurant in question also serves a great Pollo Mollo.'

'And what is that?' sneered Rupert. 'Regurgitated parrot?'

'No, Rupert. Chicken in chocolate.'

'Chicken in chocolate? Don't these fucking locals eat anything civilised?'

'Rupie! Shut up. You're pissed and beginning to make a spectacle of yourself.' Nigel took a deep breath, returning his partner's glare with equal ferocity while Mike sat calmly surveying the two, a smile playing on his full mouth. 'Either you take yourself up to the room or else you order a coffee and try and get yourself into some semblance of sobriety!'

'Ooh, 'ark at 'er!' cooed Rupert camply. He stood up unsteadily. 'If you'll excuse me, Miss Mary!' he hissed at a still smiling Mike (the smile quickly disappearing) 'I had better leave as this Mary can certainly tell when she's no longer wanted on the voyage!' With that he made his way sedately towards the bar entrance, narrowly missing a table of drinkers on his way out.

'Sorry about that, Mike,' said Nigel, forcing a smile. 'I've never seen Rupie behave quite like this before. It's so out of character!'

'Put it down to the altitude and too many pisco sours,' laughed Mike. 'A lethal combination!'

'So I've noticed,' responded Nigel drily.

Mike pointed at their empty glasses. 'One for the road and then dinner?'

'Why not,' said Nigel as Mike beckoned the waiter over.

'How long have you two been together?' asked Mike. The two, having satiated themselves on the aforesaid roasted guinea pig and consumed two bottles of the now familiar Torrontes were on their final brandies. He gave Nigel a searching look. 'Not that I'm prying but I am always curious as to how two guys, so different, actually get together and go through that final commitment? I mean, don't get me wrong, I know opposites attract but you and Rupert are, well, so very, very different.'

Nigel and Rupert had earlier assessed that, according to Rupert 'Mike was one of us' and Mike, in his turn had made this quite clear by saying during their earlier lunch, 'It's good to see two guys like yourselves so happy together,' and, on being questioned about his own status had simply replied, 'Oh, I'm a bona fide loner. My attitude is and has always been "find 'em, fuck 'em and forget 'em!"'

Nigel gave a laugh. 'You mean a boring old fart like me and a ravishing young thing like Rupie? No, don't be embarrassed, Mike, I know what you mean.' He leant conspiratorially across the table. 'I was late coming out. I met Rupie at some party and I was fascinated by someone so openly gay and so unconcerned and natural about it. He is, apart from my first attempt at a gay experience, the only guy I have ever had sex with. Somehow I found a defiance encouraged by our relationship, a defiance against my family and all those bigoted people I work with. A fuck you all attitude. Accepting Rupie as part of my life seemed the natural course of events. Working even harder I became the golden boy of the company and with my financial achievements, my uncanny knack for hauling in the big fish, I can do no wrong. Rupert is more tolerated than adored but never-the-less he is de rigueur at all the business functions albeit it a cocktail party, dinner party or even a conference should he be free from his school duties.'

He paused for breath, startled by his vehement disclosure. 'I'm not criticising Rupie,' he added hastily, 'but simply saying that whatever people think, I love him and will until – as they say – "death do us part!"'

Bullshit thought Mike but said instead. 'Good on you, Nige. It's not often that one hears one so prepared to stick by his man.' He took another sip of his brandy as he eyed a startled Nigel across the rim of the glass.

Are you being sarky or what? thought Nigel. And what's with the Nige bit?

Mike glanced at the Swatch watch on his beefy wrist. 'It's getting late and I've got an early plane to catch. Pity the two of you are staying on for a few more days, it would have been fun to have you join me on my foray down the Amazon.'

'Another time, perhaps, Mike,' said Nigel with a relieved smile. 'Yes, I'd better get back to the hotel and check on young Rupie. Poor lad is going to have quite a hangover to cope with in the morning.'

'Lucky Rupie,' said Mike, 'waking up with you in the morning!' This being said with a lecherous grin.

'Oh well, that depends on your point of view,' said Nigel uncomfortably. 'I don't think he's all that lucky!'

'Oh no? Don't underestimate yourself Nige. You're successful, good-looking – quite a catch if I may say. Your Rupie is a very, very lucky and also a very clever guy.'

'Why clever?'

'Oh. C'mon, Nige! Look at the two of you. That young man's got it made.' He raised a placating hand. 'And before you fly off the handle, think of it. You're bound together for the rest of your lives. The rest of one's life can be a very long time indeed.' He gave the now thunderous-faced Nigel a challenging look. 'Don't try and kid me that your Rupert is the innocent, dewy-eyed ingénue you hold him out to be. You can't have missed the way he was flirting with me at lunch. Why, he even tried to grope my crotch under the table, for fuck's sake!'

'Bullshit!' An outraged Nigel jumped to his feet causing the small table to rock violently and his own glass to fall to the stone floor with a shattering crash. Flinging a wad of notes onto the table he hissed as he nodded in the direction of the dark, brooding cathedral. 'That should cover the cost of this last, fucking supper! Have a safe flight!' Giving a smirking Mike a final glare he stormed his way off across the darkened square.

'Oh Nige, dear Nige. Have I got plans for the rich, charming never-been-properly bedded you!' said Mike out loud to the departing figure. Beckoning the waiter who had hastily cleared up the broken pieces of glass, he ordered himself another brandy. 'And as for you, you pathetic little teacher troll, you are going to rue the day you called me Mary Poppins for, I can assure you this Mary Poppins is about to be a total cunt.'

The next morning as Nigel, accompanied by a very hung over Rupert (the latter hiding behind a large pair of Dolce and Gabana sunglasses) stopped by the front desk to hand in their room key, he found himself being handed a sealed envelope by the pretty receptionist.

'For you Meestah Collins,' said the girl with a dazzling smile. 'Meestah Mayhew said me to make sure you get eet!' Nigel, with his blond, Christopher Cazanove looks, had already caused a few giggles amongst the girl – and the boy – receptionists.

'Why…er… thank you.' Nigel quickly folded the envelope and stuck it into the breast pocket of his light linen jacket. To his relief, Rupert who was looking as if he was about to throw up, was otherwise distracted.

On the tourist bus en route to visit the local market in the nearby town of Pisac, Nigel – Rupert had fallen asleep again, his head against the window and his mouth hanging open, an unattractive drool of spit slowly making its way down his chin – quietly opened the envelope. The folded paper inside was blank apart from two words – Call me. A quick search inside the envelope showed it to contain a business card with Mike's telephone and mobile numbers plus an email address.

'You've got to be joking,' muttered Nigel. 'Not a hope in hell, Mike, mate!' The latter word spat out so vehemently that it caused Rupert to open one bleary, bloodshot eye.

'What?' he mumbled.

'Nothing, Rupie,' said Nigel quietly. 'I simply said we appear to be running late.'

Two weeks after their return to London Nigel, finally yielding both to temptation and a latent curiosity, rang Mike's mobile. To his relief and also to his disappointment he received the answering service. As requested, he dutifully left a message. Within five minutes Mike had responded to his call with the two arranging to meet later at the cocktail bar in Flemings Hotel in Mayfair, a regular haunt of Nigel's.

Nigel, to his dismay had arrived exactly at the scheduled time only to find the luxuriously appointed cocktail bar almost empty apart from table of two American couples talking loudly about their disappointment with their viewing of Buckingham Palace.

'It looks like a giant dump!' grizzled one.

'A dump is a dump!' grizzled another, obviously not best pleased with one of London's most popular 'must sees.'

'Really, Toots!' chided one of the party, a much-lifted, deeply tanned, bleached matron in her late sixties, seventies or maybe more.

'Well, it's what I think!' replied Toots sulkily.

Any further eavesdropping on the riveting conversation was interrupted by the arrival of a beaming Mike. 'Sorry I'm late, Nige!' he announced breezily, slipping onto the low banquette alongside the other man. 'I was breaking in a new client!' He gave a lascivious wink, 'If you know what I mean!' He pointed at Nigel's glass. 'What's that you're drinking? A Martini? Vodka? Good, I'll have one of those as well.' He smiled up at the equally smiling waiter. 'And make it a large one.'

The innuendo did not go unnoticed by Nigel. Oh no, he groaned inwardly, maybe this is a mistake. Instead he said brightly to the hovering barman. 'Make that two, please Cruise. Thank you.' He lent back against the comfortable upholstery, looking at the grinning man seated next to him, becoming immediately aware of an almost, animal-like musk drifting his way. Jesus, he smells of sex and sweat, he thought, his groin beginning to react accordingly. Don't tell me the filthy bastard has come straight here after a screw without taking a shower?

As if reading his thoughts Mike lifted his arm and sniffed surreptitiously at his armpit. 'Oops! A bit ripe. Sorry about that, Nige! Couldn't wait to get the old condom off, the old knickers on and get round here to see you. Fresh from this morning though so it's not too bad!'

Jesus, you filthy, fucking pig! Was Nigel's immediate thought. He gave a slight grimace and moved slightly away from the still grinning man, a move which was ignored. 'So, how was the Amazon?' he asked, for want of something to say and breaking the silence which had now descended on the two of them, Mike still grinning at him like a predatory Cheshire Cat.

'Wide.' Said Mike reaching for his Martini from the proffered tray. 'But more interesting, how is London town treating you and are you still making lots and lots of money?' He gave a laugh. 'Don't look so surprised. I did a check up on you when I got back, quite the golden boy aren't you? What is it they call you? The Man with the Midas Touch or something in that golden vein!' Mike laughed heartily at his wit.

'You did a check up on me?' Nigel looked at Mike incredulously. 'A check up? Why for God's sake?'

'Why? Because you seem almost too good to be true, Nige, that's why!' Mike took a long sip of his drink while giving the other man the shrewdest of looks. 'How's that drunken faggoty friend of yours, by the way? Robert? Ronald?'

'You know bloody well he's called Rupert and I resent you referring to him as my faggoty friend. In fact,' here Nigel swallowed the rest of his replacement drink. 'I should have known better. Meeting up with you has been a mistake. And Mike, do have another. I run a permanent tab here.'

'Here we go!' sang Mike, still grinning his irrefutable grin. 'Cuzco all over again!'

Nigel stopped in mid-stride. Turning to glare at the seated man he snapped. 'What does that mean, Cuzco all over again?'

'Well, you stormed off in a queenly huff when I criticised your nearest and dearest and now you're doing it again!'

Nigel stood looking down at Mike. 'What is it exactly you have against Rupert? You know he's my lover and yes, I do object most strongly to you slagging him off the way you have been doing on the two occasions when we have met!' Nigel, now fuming, seemed impervious to the fascinated looks from the four Americans who were no doubt finding this scenario far more rewarding than Buckingham Palace.

'Oh, sit down for fuck's sake, Nige and have another drink.' Mike turned and gave the four gaping tourists a wider grin. 'Fascinating enough for you? The conversation I mean.'

'Well, really!' said a flustered 'Toots,' his face reddening. 'Well really.' Within moments the four had exited from the bar leaving a still standing Nigel glowering down at the maddeningly calm Mike. Mike beckoned over the ever vigilant Cruise. 'The same again, please. On my bill. Not on Mr Collins's.'

Against his will Nigel found himself compelled to sit. He was just about to make some excuse for not having another drink when any potential conversation was drowned out by a loud cheerful, glamorous group sweeping into the bar. Cries of 'Evening Cruise' followed by another of 'Two bottles of the house bubbly tout de suite, please!' cut through the frosty atmosphere.

'Why don't we finish these and go back to my place where I can fuck your brains out?'

A startled Nigel looked wild-eyed at Mike. 'What did you just say?'

'You heard. Come back to the flat and let me fuck you!' Mike lifted his half-finished drink. 'I bet in all your time with Rupert he's never fucked you, in fact, if I'm not mistaken Nige, you've never, ever been fucked!'

Nigel's face was now deep crimson, his throat choked with further embarrassment.

'Let me guess,' continued Mike relentlessly. 'Always the fuckee and never the one fucked?' He shook his head, another grin spreading across his mischievous face. 'Tsk! Tsk! Nige. You don't know what you've been missing!' He looked up at the barman. 'Thanks, Cruise. And the bill please, Mr Collins and I have just remembered we have an important previous appointment!'

Nigel looked wild around the now noisy, crowded bar. Was it his imagination or was Mike's powerful, animal-like musk becoming more apparent? Feeling the start of a gigantic erection, the likes of which he'd never experienced before, he swallowed dryly. 'You'll have to excuse me. I told Rupert I'd be home in time for us to go out to dinner...' his voice petering out, leaving a heavy silence.

'Late night at the office, Nige. That's the only excuse or excusing you'll need to use this evening. C'mon, drink up.' Mike nodded his head in the direction of Nigel's bulging crotch. 'If we don't do something about him soon you're going to have to explain a pair of very messy trousers to your innocent Rupie and, knowing Rupie, Miss Very Queer, she will not be amused!'

'Why you...!'

'Why you what, Nige? C'mon man, you're gagging for it and, if I'm to be honest about it, I wanted to fuck you from the moment I saw you on top of that peak at Machu Pichu. Mary bloody Poppins indeed. Much, much more Macho Poppins – if you get my drift!'

Half an hour later after a tense taxi ride in which Mike sat slouched away from a frustrated Nigel on the opposite side of the cab, the two barely made it through the front door to Mike's duplex flat in Chelsea's elegant Redcliffe Square. Within seconds the two men were standing in the expansive sitting room, both naked, both panting and both hungrily eyeing each other and their rampant erections. 'The bedroom's up through here,' said Mike hoarsely grabbing Nigel by the cock and leading him to the stairs up to the next floor. Once inside the room Mike threw Nigel roughly onto the king size bed, his eyes glittering cruelly. 'Oh Nige,' he said, stroking his own formidable length. 'Are you going to be well and truly broken in, mate! I tell you, you are about to be well and truly fucked!'

'You can't seriously be thinking of putting that inside me?' questioned Nigel tremulously. 'It's a fucking monster!'

'Oh, so you've noticed, have you?' Mike gave a laugh as he leaned across, his arm stretching out towards the bedroom table. 'I'm not into foreplay this evening, Nige. I think it important you immediately find out what you've been missing all these years. Foreplay can come later!' Unwrapping a condom he unrolled it up his pulsating, red swollen shaft but not before pulling back the heavy foreskin. 'Glad to see you're not cut, Nige,' he whispered. 'Later I'll show you what a nibble on the old foreskin can do for you!' He gave a grunt as he lifted a now resigned Nigel's legs onto his shoulders. Squeezing a generous amount of lubricant onto the fingers of his right hand he then slowly began to press first one finger and then two into Nigel's hot, excessive taut, tight arsehole. 'Relax, Nige,' Mike whispered hoarsely. 'Relax!'

'It hurts,' whimpered Nigel, clenching his jaw. 'Christ, that hurts. I can't Mike! Please stop! I can't!'

'There's no such word as can't!' growled Mike deftly twisting his two fingers inside the now loosened opening. Without any further hesitation he plunged his full, turgid length deeply into the now receptive Nigel. After the first few powerful thrusts Nigel's whimpers changed to deep throated grunts of pleasure. As Mike increased the speed and power of his thrusts Nigel began to masturbate himself furiously. Within seconds he felt the start of the most sensational orgasm and before he could stop himself he began ejaculating wildly over Mike's pumping, pounding chest.

'Me too! Me too!' bellowed Mike as he spurted into the now laughing, sobbing man beneath him. 'Christ, Nige! Christ! You're a fucking marvel!'

After three repeat performances involving bouts of fellatio and more ardent fucking – Mike had allowed Nigel to mount him only to find Nigel stopping after a few minutes and insisting they reverse roles – the two exhausted, satiated men lay side by side on the twisted, sweaty sheets, a large drink each in their hands.

'So?' asked a grinning Mike, his hand softly fondling Nigel's now flaccid, long, thick cock.

'So what?' A smiling Nigel turned and kissed the other man lightly on his tanned cheek.

'So what is it like to have been so brutally deflowered at the tender age of thirty plus?'

'Fucking fantastic!' came the laughing reply. Nigel glanced down at his Rolex on the black lacquered bedside cabinet alongside him. 'Jesus! Is that the time? I'd better be going! Office or no office it being after two in the morning is going to take some explaining.'

'Oh Nige! Oh Nige!' cooed Mike camply from the bed as the anxious man began to make his way quickly out of the bedroom door towards the stairs.

'Yes?'

'May I suggest a shower afore ye go?' Mike gave a laugh. 'If you thought I was a tad ripe on arrival at Flemings the two of us are now more like a couple of rancid pole cats. Boysie woysie Rupie will not be amused!'

Nigel took a quick sniff at his armpit. 'Christ! I didn't think.' His face broke into a beatific smile. 'Buggers' BO!' he laughed. He nodded towards a closed door. 'The bathroom?'

'It's all yours.' Mike gave a yawn and a long stretch. 'I'll nip downstairs and bring your clobber up for you. I'll then see you back down in the sitting room.' He nodded towards the empty wine glass. 'A quick one for the road? A brandy perhaps?'

'Why not?' said Nigel striding laughingly towards the bathroom door. 'In for a penny, in for a pounding! If I'm going to get a bollocking I might as well be pissed for the occasion!'

'Atta boy!' laughed Mike. 'I'll see you downstairs.'

A besotted Nigel eagerly met up with Mike at his flat a few days later, a meeting which saw the start of many such clandestine arrangements. Nigel and Rupert, living in a spacious, detached Georgian house in Richmond, meant the break in the journey between Richmond and the City was made easier for Nigel in what had become a regular rendezvous. Breaking his journey at Earls Court he was able to be at Mike's flat in a matter of minutes.

After the initial bouts of what seemed to be insatiable sex the two slipped into the comfortable routine of meeting, having sex and then walking up to the local Balans restaurant on the corner of Redcliffe Gardens and the Old Brompton Road for a late supper. The restaurant, a popular gay venue, proved a welcome respite to Nigel's otherwise rigid social life which appeared to revolve around business and more business. Mike had shown little surprise on hearing that Rupert preferred either staying in or else meeting a few friends locally.

Fucking little Dora domestic! he had thought uncharitably on hearing this gem of information.

It was during one of their late suppers that Mike broached the topic of their relationship. 'This civil partnership of yours, Nige, what does it involve exactly?'

'Simple,' had been the reply. 'Everything I have goes to Rupie should anything unfortunate happen to me and vice versa.'

'Everything?'

Nigel took mouthful of his rib eye steak. After a moment of concentrated chewing he went on. 'I have no family which means Rupie is my family. His parents, bless them, are still alive and live down on the coast near to Bournemouth. They worship their son and yes, before you ask, they know he's gay – he told them years ago.'

Told them? thought Mike cruelly. They'd have to be fucking blind not to see they'd produced a screaming parakeet of a queen for a son!

'So, our Rupert is an heiress in waiting?' Mike couldn't help a snigger at his comment.

'Well, he's got quite a wait,' laughed Nigel. He gave Mike's hand a firm squeeze under the table. 'Now I've got you in my life, Mikey, I'm not planning on leaving for the upper echelon just yet!'

'How serious are you when you say something like that?' Mike's expression and question causing Nigel to look at him in surprise.

'Why, you er… know what I mean, Mike.' He gave a nervous smile. 'Over the past few weeks I've grown extremely fond of you. In fact, I couldn't imagine my life without you…' His voice trailed off into silence. 'Why?' he asked again softly.

Mike let out a long sigh. 'Oh Nigel, what am I to do with you?' He gave the man a soft, sad smile. 'Do you remember what I said to you at our first dinner together back in Cuzco? My motto?'

'Yes, Mikey, I do. I must admit I was a bit shocked at the time by what you said.'

'Yes, "find 'em, fuck 'em and forget 'em!" is what I said that night. Well Nige, that's all changed.' He sat for a moment staring at Nigel who, not knowing what was coming next, began to toy nervously with the stem of his wine glass. Lowering his voice he leaned across the table. 'Now I think I'd prefer to say "I've found you, love to fuck you and never want to forget you!"'

Nigel knocked over his glass of wine which fortunately was almost empty. 'Jesus Mike!' he uttered, his face ashen. 'Please, please don't say that.'

'But why not, Nige, when I mean it?'

'But I'm already involved with Rupie!'

'No, Nige, you're not involved with Rupert, you feel yourself under an obligation to him!' Mike gave a frustrated shrug of his broad shoulders. 'Be honest Nige, you've almost but admitted it. Rupert was basically the only gay experience you had had until you met me! Let's face it, when we first went to bed you were a novice. To you sex was lying on top of someone's back while he lay on his stomach! Jesus, when I first took you doggie fashion you thought you'd died and gone to Crufts!'

The crack about the world famous dog show broke the tension with Nigel laughing a bit too loudly at the joke. 'You had me really worried there for a moment, Mikey, really worried. Here, let's have another of these before I go and catch my train.'

As they waited for Daniel, their handsome, chunky waiter to fetch their drinks – Mike always referred to Daniel as 'Mr Sex on Legs' – Mike couldn't resist the question to end all questions. 'Forgive me for asking, Nige, but what exactly does Rupert think of the new Nigel in bed?'

'Think? Why, what should he think?' Nigel gave a hollow laugh. 'We haven't had sex for at least two weeks and when we did I made damn sure it was stomach down and me on his back!'

'Not only a handsome face but a wise one to boot,' said Mike approvingly.

'Something I was about to ask you,' continued Nigel, his relief at the change of subject being paramount. 'Rupie's off to visit his parents this weekend and I was wondering what you'd say to a weekend in Richmond?'

'You mean, a weekend in your home sweet home?' Mike gave an almost evil laugh. 'Naughty, naughty Nigel. Why I do believe this is a case of while the cat's away our Nige plans to play.'

'You're absolutely bloody right!' laughed Nigel looking thoroughly pleased with himself, 'Absolutely bloody fucking absolutely right!'

As Rupert was due to visit his parents on the Friday the two arranged to meet at Balans for a light supper – 'No raping until Richmond!' had been Nigel's laughing instructions – before taking the train to their destination. 'Just bring a change of underwear and a couple of T shirts,' he had also said. 'And as it looks as if it's to be a scorcher we'll probably spend most of our time in the pool.'

'You have a pool?'

'Oh shit, Mikey, I should have told you, the house is quite something. Not only have we a pool but we have a tennis court and a cinema, never mind an indoor gym you'll more than likely go nuts over.' Nigel, in his enthusiasm and resultant lack of tact did not notice the dark look cast in his direction at this unintentional boasting.

We have! We have! It's all this fucking we have that's doing my head in and it's that little shit who is going to benefit from all of this! The sentence and thought was now repeating itself time and time again like a mantra in Mike's mind. Nigel, in a moment of post coital confession had mentioned to Mike his worrying heart condition, not once, but twice, plus his concern as to how Rupert would cope if 'the worse came to the worst.' It did not take Mike long to make a decision. Speaking out loud in the privacy of the bathroom he had vowed to his mirrored reflection. 'All of his success? That little turd is to get it all?' Giving a hollow laugh Mike had then assured his glaring double. 'No way, Rupie baby, no way are you going to get it all. Not if I have anything to do with it!'

The house in Richmond was even more grand than Mike could have imagined. 'Christ Nige,' he said as they lay together in the large airy bedroom, a bottle of champagne in an ice bucket next to them. 'How much does a place like this set one back? Simply an approximate figure will do.'

'In today's market about three.'

'Three hundred thousand? Christ!' Mike decided to play dumb.

'No Mikey said Nigel with a friendly chuckle. 'Three million!'

Next day Mike was even more intrigued to see both a Mercedes coupe and a gleaming BMW saloon sitting side by side in the spacious garage. 'His and hers,' he sniped sarcastically.

'Absolutely!' laughed Nigel, refusing to rise to the jibe. 'Only Rupie doesn't drive his Merc that often nowadays.' He gave Mike an embarrassed smile. 'He seems to be drinking more since we returned from our trip and therefore inclined to get somewhat dangerously pissed when out.' He gave a self-deprecating chuckle. 'Therefore it's up to solid, reliable Nigel to do the driving. Besides, Rupie has never taken the car when he goes down to visit his parents as both Mr and Mrs Landau have a penchant for their Gs and Ts and encourage their son to join in!'

Like parents, like daughter, thought Mike harshly. He glanced at Nigel standing alongside him. Maybe little Rupie should get out more is his little Noddy car! Now there's an idea…

SEVEN MONTHS LATER:

Mike looked up at the closed bedroom door. 'You can come in now,' he called. 'It's all done.'

'Is he dead?'

'No problem. The potassium cyanide worked like a dream although – for him – not a sweet one!' Mike gave a cynical grin. 'Now a decent time of mourning and then it's our turn to tie the knot!' He gave another grin, this one decidedly genuine. 'Perfect planning even if I say it myself.'

'As I said to you before we met up as planned in Peru, you're a fucking genius Mikey!'

Rupert looked down at the supine figure on the bed before turning back to a still grinning Mike. 'Poor Nigel. The old sod would have had an even earlier, genuine heart attack had he any idea as to what we had been planning all along.' He held out his arms. 'Welcome home, lover!'

'Touché!' replied Mike, his grin getting wider as he stood thinking. Touché indeed, you little shit. Oh dear little Rupie, if only you knew. Twelve months max of your shit and then a nice little car crash and Mikey gets all. Yes, sweetheart, as I said before and I say it again with embellishments; your dear devoted Machu Mary Poppins is nothing more than a total unmitigated, mercenary, evil scheming cunt!

'A drink to celebrate?' he added. giving the smiling Rupert a tender kiss on his parted lips.

ENGLISHMAN WANTA JOIN IN!

Peter Davis smiled indulgently, condescendingly, sarcastically or simply downright patronisingly – take your pick – at his two dinner guests before blowing out a perfect smoke ring, aided and abetted by his extravagant, aromatic Davidoff cigar.

'Sooo, you wish to see a sex show?' He allowed himself an even greater, ingratiating, superior smile, his well-combed eyebrow raising itself questioningly. 'How very touristy!'

'Well, it just so happens we are tourists, Peter, and this is our first visit to Bangkok!' Mark Witherspoon looked irritatedly at the rotund, jowly, pink face of his former school friend. Christ, what a smug, self-satisfied, fat prick you've become, Peter Davis! he thought before saying out loud, 'And as Bangkok is well known for all sorts of strange, sexual divertissements – and as you are obviously some sort of a Wikipedia seeing you live here, who else would one ask?'

Davis gave an even greater – if possible – self-indulgent smile. 'But of course! And I know just the place! Let's finish our brandies on the veranda and then I'll get Li, my driver to take your there.' He gave another smile – or smirk – before adding. 'And before you ask, no, I won't be joining you – it's a bit passé for me that sort of thing – but no doubt you'll both enjoy it!' He stood up, brandy balloon in his beefy, pink, hairless hand. 'And again, don't worry about getting back to your hotel. Li will wait for you. It's what he's paid for!' He gave another laugh. 'I may even have an old number for the place and give them a ring on your behalf.'

'What an arsehole!' Malcolm Mayhew, Mark's lover of five year's standing, gave a brief laugh, squeezing his partner's knee affectionately. He nodded his boyish head towards the tiny, silent Li sitting upright behind the wheel of the large Mercedes and craning to peer over the dashboard while nurturing the car along at a sedate, stately speed. 'Do you think he's listening and going to report back to Billy Bunter?'

'So what?' laughed Mark drily. 'It's what he's paid for!' he added in a perfect take-off of Peter's nasal, high pitched, affected voice.

'God, I love you Mark!' whispered Malcolm, squeezing his friend's knee once again. 'And thanks again for bringing me here... A life long dream come true!'

Mark, a tall, dark-haired, good-looking man, well built and in his early forties, looked down affectionately at the blond, slightly built, twenty six year old sitting next to him. 'No, thank you, Molky, for being you and allowing me to help you fulfil – and be part of – that dream.'

'Oh, you've fulfilled all my dreams – in many ways! In fact, you keep on fulfilling them, awake or in the land of nod!' Malcolm gave a small sigh. 'I still cannot believe it'll be five years tomorrow; five years since we literally bumped into each other in Waitrose on that wet, windy Saturday morning! (Mark, intensely studying the racks of greens in the vegetable section of the exclusive King's Road store had pushed his shopping trolley unsuspectingly into an equally contemplative Malcolm standing and surveying a bank of bagged Brussels sprouts).

'Five years tomorrow and fifty more to go,' smiled Mark. He nodded towards the window and the seedy, dimly lit passing street. 'Christ! This place is a shithole! If it weren't for a few fabulous, completely-out-of-context temples and our hotel (they were ensconced in a suite courtesy of the luxurious Shangri-La Hotel overlooking the busy Chao Phraya river), forget it!'

'The floating market was fun!'

'The floating market, my dear Molky, is not Bangkok!' Mark gave a hollow laugh. 'Let's hope this show is up to scratch but, having met the reborn Peter Davis and his latest penchant for oriental takeaway chicken – that pretty, painted youth tripping daintily from the house just as we arrived – was, from what I could gather, more egg than chicken!' Giving a resigned grin he added, 'It'll probably be more a Peter's paedophile paradise than a proper pervert's pornographic one!'

'Put it down to experience!' laughed Malcolm. 'Oh! We seem to have stopped!' He peered into a gloomy alleyway adjacent to his side of the now stationary car. 'Not quite Soho, is it?' He turned his gaze back to Li who was now looking at them, eyes blank and uncompromising. 'This the place, Li?'

'Downa stleet! Housa wit blue lite!'

'Blue lamp as opposed to red?' Mark gave a snigger. 'Well, I suppose it is the mysterious East!'

'You wait, Li?' This from Malcom.

'Shure boss! Li wait. Showa vella good! Vella good! Vella naughty!' The little driver gave a giggle. 'Mista Petah allus enjoy!'

'I thought "Mista Petah" deemed such places as passé even though he just happened to have the number in his little pink book!' commented Mark as the two made their way up the dark, narrow litter-strewn narrow street. 'Ah, the infamous blue lamp beckons.' They stopped in front of a small, narrow door (also blue) alongside the dimly glowing light. 'It gets better and better,' he added. 'No buzzer, only a sliding hatch. So, intrepid lover, I gather we're supposed to knock!'

'Well,' said Malcolm, with a low chuckle. 'It is some sort of knocking shop!'

'That, Molky, does not become you!'

The small hatch slid open to reveal a bloodshot, rheumy eye set in what appeared to be an old walnut. 'Yus?'

'Er... we've come to see the show.

'Hah! Englisha flend Mista Peetah!'

With that the hatch quickly slid closed and, after a few seconds of bolts being thrown, the door was opened to display a small, bald, yellow, wizened old man dressed incongruously in an old fashioned dinner jacket, complete with evening shirt and black bow tie, all set atop a pair of drooping shorts and a pair of skinny legs proudly boasting a pair of mismatched shoes. 'Plis!' said the little man, smiling and displaying a mouthful of gleaming gold teeth. 'Plis, Enta Housa Dleems. I ama Sinsam, yoha host!'

Joel Grey, eat your heart out! As if reading Mark's mind a cracked recording of Liza Minnelli singing the theme from Cabaret came creeping eerily through the dim blue light of the small entry lobby.

'It's Bob Fosse meets Suzie Wong!' giggled Mark. He nodded towards the little man. 'Our very own oriental version of Joel Grey if you catch my drift.'

'Enta! Enta!' The bobbing, grinning little man gave an extravagant gesture towards a larger room just visible through the gloom. 'Dlinks ona Mistah Peetah. Plis. Bar leddy for you!' Still bobbing, Sinsam backed towards the bar before turning round and clucking in a series of high pitched croaks. 'Light! BK! Dlinks for honnahed guests!'

Mark, not daring to look across at Malcolm also doing his best to stifle any laughter, managed to hiss through the side of his twitching mouth. 'Messrs Maugham and Greene, eat your hearts out. This atmosphere is pure Rain and there, slumped against the bar is your archetypal sozzled, despairing, lonely English ex pat.' His mouth twitched even more. 'Better watch out, Molky, Mr MG over there could just see you as his very own Sadie Thompson?'

'Mr MG? Rain? Sadie Thompson? I don't follow you. Joel Grey was just catchable!'

'I'll explain later. Ah, yes Sinsam.' He smiled again at his still sniggering lover (the man slumped at the bar meanwhile giving them both a bleary, narrow-eyed drunken stare). 'What are you drinking Molky, Sinsam is getting restless!'

'Oh, a G and T please.' He turned to the still bobbing little man. 'That's a gin and tonic, please er…Sinsam.'

His use of Sinsam's name was rewarded by a loud cackle and a further flashing of gold dentures. 'En you sah?' This to Mark.

'A beer please, Sinsam.'

'Pliss!' Sinsam gestured proudly towards the bar counter where the barman – an equally grinning, bald-headed youth was rapidly seeing to their orders having had these croaked across the small bar area by the cheerful, impish master-of-ceremonies, inn keeper or brothel keeper, whichever role Sinsam was professing to be. He pointed proudly towards the still grinning young man. 'My son Big Knob! He too in show!'

'Christ!' muttered Mark. 'A fucking family affair to boot!' He lifted his large glass of Singha beer (a popular, local brew) in a toast to his lover, with Malcolm raising a similarly very large glass of gin and tonic in return. 'What next, I wonder?' he murmured. 'Perhaps Big Knob now does just that? Simply shows us the family jewels!'

'Pliss? You follow Sinsam?' The little man, still bobbing energetically and grinning wildly, beckoned with a skinny hand, the jacket of his well worn dinner jacket sleeve falling back to display not one but two gold Rolexes dangling on his bony wrist.

'Obviously Housa Dleems makes plenty Amelican dolla!' giggled Malcolm.

'Shush, dearest! We don't want a rampant Big Knob out to avenge a slight on the family's good name, now do we? Or do we?'

'Quite right, lover! Perhaps we simply wait and ogle the mighty source of the Rolexes instead!' He smiled at Sinsam. 'Lead on, Macduff!'

'Pliss?'

'Scottish for "After you," Sinsam!'

With another flash of his gold dentures the sprightly little man shuffled importantly to the start of a small staircase adjacent to the bar and leading up to a gloomy first floor. Dutifully following him Mark and Malcolm's exit was accompanied by a loud wet fart from the shabby drinker at the bar, closely followed by a similar, sloppy second.

'Thanks for the send off, *Again Sam!*' sniggered Mark.

'Again Sam? Is this another of your erudite asides?' This from a grimacing Malcolm at the sound of the second slippery phut.

'Almost! Think Casablanca only Sam was requested to *play* it again!'

Malcolm shook his head, giving the smiling Mark a fond look. 'I give up...' he began, only to be interrupted by Sinsam's excited, 'Lookie! Lookie!'

Pulling open another viewing hatch to a firmly closed door, the little man pointed excitedly towards the aperture. 'Lookie! Lookie!' He insisted again, his wrinkled face wreathed in mischievous smiles.

Both Mark and Malcolm peered in as commanded. Mark's burst of laughter was contagious. 'Jesus, Molky, get a load of that!' He glanced down at the grinning little man. 'Honestly Joel!' (The reference to the master of ceremonies was to stick).

Seeing their amusement their host quickly reasserted himself. 'Ah, no, no. no! This lookie, lookie onla! Sex show upastair!'

Giving the little man both a bemused and disbelieving smile, the two men peered back into the small, grubby, dimly lit room, the first of five more in which the other shows would be similarly viewed before the big show 'upastair' would be revealed.

Kneeling on his all fours, a stark naked elderly man – a look of intense concentration on his face as he studied what could only be a luridly illustrated pornographic magazine – was busily having his skinny shanks pummelled by a large, bright pink plastic dildo held by an equally frowning and deeply concentrating youth. The harder the youth pummelled the flashing dildo in and out, the more intense became the old man's studying. What made the scene even more incongruous was the pornographic magazine leaning against its own wooden stand leaving the old man with his hands free, one helping to support himself while the other was laconically masturbating an alarmingly long, pale penis. Mark exploded into further laughter when the old man momentarily removed his hand from his long, pale member and neatly turned the page before returning to his sombre ministrations.

'More lookie, lookie!' announced the now-christened Joel proudly, pointing to a further door.

'Let's hope the old boy's a fast reader for the sake of the poor lad's arm!' chortled Malcolm.

'Better still, let's hope it's a very thin comic book!' laughed Mark.

'Maybe the old boy never comes and they continue nonstop throughout whatever hours are deemed opening hours!' giggled Malcolm.

'I have a feeling we're the opening hours,' came his lover's laughing reply. 'Once that hatch is closed the old boy carries on reading and dildo Danny probably has a cigarette break!.'

'So romantic, Marky!'

'Yes, I am, aren't I?' laughed Mark.

'Lookie! Lookie!' insisted the still bobbing, grinning Joel.

Having viewed fellatio, buggery, mutual masturbation and a youth who seemed to do nothing more than pop ping pong balls up his anus before popping them out again to accurately hit a large, tarnished bronze gong, the three eventually reached the top floor.

'Now what?' muttered Mark.

On the floor, central to the small, low room, lay a thin, mattress whose marks and stains Mark later – still laughing – compared to either 'one mighty skid mark' or 'a giant Rorschach test.' Along two sides of this 'stage' were a pair of benches upon which were seated the expectant and excited audience, a motley group of men, old, young, fat and thin. At the far end of the mattress were two upright wooden chairs to which the little man now impatiently gestured for Mark and Malcolm to sit.

Still clutching their drinks the two men dutifully did as instructed. Once they had taken up their prime positions the one and only light – a naked bulb suspended from the cracked, sagging ceiling – was switched off and a watery spotlight cast upon the so-called stage. Not to be outdone by the one and only special effect, a windup gramophone was cranked into motion and a cracked version of Offenbach's 'Orpheus in the Underworld' – better know as the Can Can – began screeching out into the dimly lit room.

'Loopee!'Loopwee! (Whoopee! Whoopee!) cried Joel. 'Show starta!'

A startled Mark and Malcolm looked disbelievingly as one of the biggest black men they had ever seen strode onto the mattress accompanied by a nubile young boy. Without further ado the boy was picked up and impaled onto the black giant's even more giant erection. Hopping about to the beat of the scratchy tune the man, in turn, bounced the boy like a toy rubber doll up and down his rigid shaft. With a sudden cry he lifted the grinning boy high in his massive hands above his glistening head, before ejaculating with huge jets of hurtling cum all across the aforesaid mattress. Without a break the next act – three boys who seemed to bounce about on each other with excited cries and not doing much else – was then followed by two young men who proceeded to stuff each other with bananas taken from an actual branch of the fruit plopped down on the mucky mattress. When each had managed to shove five bananas up their plump, shiny, highly polished rears they went on to make their way around the two benches, obligingly plopping out a banana to ten lucky recipients.

'Jesus!' whispered Mark. 'I now know a new version of a Banana Split!'

'Marky!' snorted Malcolm. 'Show some respect for this mighty feast of talent before you. Oh no! Now what! Good heavens! Why I do believe it's our friendly barman, Big Knob, and by Christ! It is!'

A smiling Big Knob, his enormous erection bobbing hypnotically at a perfect forty five degree angle, stood for a moment before gesturing to another youth standing by holding what appeared to be a wicker basket. With a nimble leap the lad handed over the receptacle, opening up the lid as he did so. With a quick dip of his brawny hand Big Knob reached into the basket and withdrew a squawking, desperate-looking chicken.

'He's not…' began Malcolm.

'He is!' answered Mark.

'Oh shit!' muttered Malcolm. 'I don't somehow think this is quite what you meant by Peter Davis liking chicken!'

'I second that!' Mark gave a grimace accompanied by a loud 'Ouch!' as the chicken, giving an extra loud squawk, was deftly impaled by BK or Big Knob on his aforesaid big knob! He turned suddenly on hearing an excited, almost hysterical whispering emanating from Joel.

'What?' asked Mark noticing that Malcolm had been leaning over towards the little man as if saying something to him. To both his and Malcolm's consternation the little man, without a second's hesitation, jumped onto the mattress alongside Big Knob still busily masturbating himself with the aid of the now resigned and softly cawing chicken.

'Stopa show! Stopa show!' cried Joel, his voice breaking with excitement. 'Englisha man wanta join in! Englisha man wanta join in!'

'Oh God no!' cried a horrified Malcolm. 'I said I want another gin!'

MONSIEUR BOVARY

His mother called him 'My darling blond angel' while his stepfather
– never to her, of course – called him an insidious 'little queer!'

'Fucking little shirt-lifter!' he'd announce on several occasions to
his best friend David Maloney. 'Christ, when I fell for her I had no idea of
the baggage I was taking on. Her darling, precious Julian had been living
with his grandmother while my wife-to-be was sorting out her late husband's
business affairs. She'd hinted at a child from her former marriage, a son, and
while I expected a son like all sons, I never expected that!'

The stepfather, John Masterton, chairman of a major investment
company 'in the City' would – when alone with the frail, effeminate young
boy – regard and regale the blond, fey Julian with open, and sometimes
vociferous contempt. Comments ranging from 'And how is Miss Julia
today?' to 'Fancy a game of rugger? I am sure we could find you a big
rugger bugger to deal with you in the scrum!' would be accompanied along
with cruel, sardonic laughter, often reducing the trembling boy to tears.

'That's right, bawl your bloody little eyes out, Miss Julia,' John
Masterton would growl in his deep 'from the balls' baritone, a compliment
to his massive, hirsute frame. Such scenes inevitably ended with his stepfather spitting out with contempt the most damning suggestion of all, 'Or
better still, why not go and tell mummy precious?' while knowing full well

Julian would never have the courage to do so. While he may have been his mother's 'blond angel' in her eyes, her new, virile, powerful, 'all man' husband could do no wrong and therefore she would refuse to hear the slightest criticism regarding him. To put it bluntly, Daphne Masterton had never, ever, been so gloriously fucked in the way a growling, sweaty John Masterton fucked her in virtually what had become a daily, early morning ritual and most nights as well. This regular, early morning fuck was eagerly referred to by the boastful John as his three S's routine. 'I start with wild sex, then go on to have a satisfying shit followed by a soothing shower!'

At her husband's insistence – and much to wife's initial dismay – Julian was despatched as soon as possible to become a junior border to a harsh private school recommended by the ever obliging David Maloney whose own nephew – 'A filthy queer in the making if ever I saw one!' – had been packed off to the same seat of learning.

'He went there a boy homo and came out a man!' David assured a disinterested John Masterton whose only comment in return was the succinct 'As far as I'm concerned they can bugger the little bastard to buggery and then he can bugger off somewhere else, as long as it's out of my sight!'

To both his stepfather and his mother's amazement – and in her case, relief – a new, confident Julian seemed to immediately emerge from the shy, reclusive boy. However, unbeknown to his parents the young boy had become an instant, firm favourite of the head prefect in his house, a strapping youth named Thomas, whose prowess on the rugby field was legendary. The promise of a virile 'rugger bugger' duly fulfilled had been inadvertently followed by Thomas and Julian's own version of sex, shit and shower, again on a daily basis. No doubt Julian, if ever questioned, would have argued that he and not his mother was the happier of the two recipients. 'My stepfather's nothing more than a huge, lumbering, sweaty, stinking pig,' he would repeatedly confide to Thomas as he lay held lovingly in the strong, smooth, muscular arms of his lover, his blond head pressed against the other schoolboy's softly rising smooth, hairless, muscular chest.

With Thomas as his known protector, Julian simply blossomed out into a charming and confident young person. He was delighted to discover too a formerly hidden quick wit and to be considered as highly amusing by both his tutors and classmates. Unbeknown to him, his quick put downs were of the highest camp and it was not long before Julian found himself billed as the school's Noel Coward On joining the Dramatic Society, he became the darling of Juno Hudson, the flamboyant ex-actress wife of the headmaster.

'You should consider a future in television,' she would repeatedly tell the doting Julian. 'Make yourself a more classy version of that irritating what's-his-name? Graham something-or-other! God knows, today's television could certainly do with a bit of class. Camp and classy! That's how I see you, Julian!'

Words such as 'camp' and 'gay' were like music to Julian's young ears. Juno would liberally sprinkle her conversations with the words 'gay,' 'queen,' camp' and the even more startling, new glamorous word 'tranny.' To Juno's delight her new found protégé shone as Hamlet's Ophelia, stunned the Parents' Day audience with his outrageously over-the-top (and ravishingly pretty) Gwendolyn Fairfax in The Importance of Being Earnest and was sensational in the comedy role as the gawky Miss Gossage ('call me sausage!') in John Dighton's The Happiest Days of Our Lives.'

'And they are!' Julian would repeatedly remind Douglas, Thomas's successor (Thomas by now having gone up to Oxford) as they lay entwined after a hearty bout of sweaty sex on the shabby, broken-down sofa in Douglas's study.

Having cringingly witnessed Julian's debut performance as the fair Ophelia, James Masterton adamantly refused to attend any more Parents' Day or other school functions, making a last minute business meeting the usual excuse. Once, to add conviction to his regular absences he went so far as to travel to New York for a few days. Little did Daphne Masterton know that her husband's busty, brunette secretary, the nubile Noreen Butterworth, was there – as on numerous other occasions – to take dictation! On these occasions Daphne would be happily accompanied by her close friend, Mildred Armitage, a woman described by James Masteron (again to the always listening David) as 'The most congealed cunt in Britain!'

During the summer of his first senior year, Julian was introduced by the ever enthusiastic Juno to Gustave Flaubert and Madame Bovary – 'The gayest novel ever!' she had trilled – an introduction which – like his earlier introduction to Thomas – would change his life.

In their private moments Julian would now insist on Doug calling him Emma, after Emma Bovary, Flaubert's flawed heroine. 'And you're my big butch, brawny Rodolphe Boulanger with the biggest banger – or to retain its French flavour – the biggest saucisson in the business!'

When Doug would protest weakly at yet another gift from his insatiable young lover (Daphne Masterton kept her 'angel' showered with extravagant 'Surprise! Surprise!' cheques which arrived almost weekly in their heavily scented, lilac envelopes), his protests were laughingly ignored and followed by either a blowjob or a fuck but, on most occasions, an energetic 'thank you' version of both.

'Ah!' Juilan/Emma would exclaim when receiving yet another of these distinctive carriers, 'Maybe this time a second pair of Mr Lauren's jeans for my randy Rodolphe – or why not that new mobile he keeps banging on about? His banging on being my arse's passport to paradise!'

To Doug's further delight – and here again, only in the privacy of his study – a fully made-up Julian/Emma would dress in an outrageous, twenties', sequinned flapper-styled dress inadvertently borrowed from the Dramatic Society's extensive wardrobe (a relic from an enthusiastic production of The Boy Friend in which the winsome Julian – on Juno Hudson's insistence – had played the even more winsome, simpering heroine, Polly).

'I like to see your lipstick marks on my cock!' Doug would groan looking down on the bobbing blond head, the long faux pearl necklace rattling against the to-ing and fro-ing, sequined-sparkling chest as Julian/ Emma did the honours. A few weeks later Doug's groans were to become even louder after Juilan/Emma presented him with a jewelled, adjustable gold bracelet (bought via a catalogue spotted in some fashion magazine) which, stretched to its fullest resulted in the most stimulating cock ring.

'You're too extravagant, far too extravagant,' Doug had weakly remonstrated as he surveyed his still engorged, tightly bound purple-hued cock and bulging balls. Giving a sardonic laugh, he couldn't help adding, 'You'll end up, Emma, just like your heroine and namesake, the spendthrift Madame B!'

'Just like my heroine? Just like my namesake?' Julian/Emma had squeaked, a petulant pout on his – at that particular time – red, lipstick-smeared lips. It was then he had quoted Flaubert's famous comment on being asked as to who was the inspiration behind his famous heroine, 'Madame Bovary, c'est moi!'

Daphne Masterton, having by now met Doug on several occasions, happily gave Julian her blessing for him to spend the summer holiday with the young man and his family at their villa at Cap d'Antibes. If the truth be known the woman had confessed her relief at the plan to her best friend and confidante, the always obliging, shrew-like Mildred Armitage, 'I don't think I could bear the two of them in the house together for even a day, never mind all those weeks. Darling John just cannot see eye-to-eye – never has and never will – with an artistic person like my darling, sensitive Julian.' 'No dear, of course not.' Had been the worldly-wise Mildred's dry reply. Unbeknown to Daphne, Doug's family were holidaying elsewhere (they owned a second sumptuous holiday home on Barbados) which saw the two teenagers as guests of Doug's bachelor uncle, his mother's brother, a mysterious dilettante who used the villa when the family were not in residence. On the rare occasions that they did decide to visit the South of France, Uncle Charlie would depart for a few hedonistic weeks or months to his equally lavish townhouse in Tangier. 'My Arabian night's with a K fantasy!' he would explain with a high, camp giggle.

This was to be Julian's entry into the hedonistic, rich gay set which, like platinum-plated nomads, spend their lives drifting from one exquisite watering hole to another, and, to quote Doug, 'In between constantly bitching and buggering!'

You'll adore Charlie,' he had continued. 'Charlie – or Aunt Carlotta as he prefers to be called – epitomises the phrase, Grand Old Queen! Think David Herbert, the grandest, ancient queen Tangier has ever known, apart from Barbara Hutton! – meets Carol Channing and you may just have the slightest hint of what you are about to receive!'

The meeting between Charles and Julian was an immediate case of 'love at first sight.'

'Dougie told me you were a dish but, my dear, he didn't do you justice! You're more than a mere platter! Much, much more!' Eyeing a blushing Julian he had added. 'Yes, and too, too exquisite to be wearing that shirt and those hideous shorts, whatever their labels! You, my dearly, delicious Ganymede, along with your decadent, equally malicious old auntie here' – at this stage the deeply tanned, wizened, smiling and bejewelled but alarmingly sprightly old man let out a piercing shriek before adding – 'will spend the whole holiday when we're not being fucked, in drag!' The discovery that nephew Douglas's private name for this new paragon was Emma, had led to even more delighted shrieks and the insistence that another magnum of Veuve Cliquot be opened.

Charles's live-in lover turned out to be a Moroccan of gigantic stature named Mustapha but known to all and sundry as Massivestuffa. On the following day of their arrival, Julian – now with Charles as his self-appointed wardrobe mistress, made his first appearance by the poolside in drag – or the merest suggestion of this. Dressed in a gold lame bikini, his blond hair held back by a gold and rhinestone encrusted Alice band, Julian was solemnly introduced to the assembled luncheon guests as 'Monsieur Emma Bovary.' The pseudonym was to stick. Earlier, in Charles's lavish bedroom suite while 'dressing' Julian for the forthcoming debut luncheon, the old man had let out a lascivious giggle. 'Pity about the bikini bulge, dear! More immense than Emma, if you catch my drift! Otherwise, perfection. Pure, pure perfection!'

'Touché,' had been Julian's weak response on viewing his host's tangerine hot pants, billowing, multi-hued chiffon blouse and silver stiletto strappy sandals.

'Are you ready for your big close up, Norma Emma?' cooed the little man, trembling with wicked delight.

'Norma Emma?'

'Norma Desmond, dear. Sunset Boulevard. Dear Gloria, quite her swan song!' Charles gave a shriek at his wit and, on seeing Julian's momentary baffled expression, added with a pursing of his deeply carmine-enhanced lips. 'Swanson, swan song, dear. It's a pun!'

'Get you, William Hardon!' quipped back the young man, immediately redeeming himself to a delightedly shrieking Charles.

'The daughter I've always wanted!' his beaming host warbled.

On their final day before returning to England a serious Charles (in a silk, multi-coloured Pucci trouser suit and gold Jimmy Choo sandals) put to Julian (in a pink mini dress and a pair of silver sandals on his bronzed feet, the tan showing off his pearlized toenails to perfection) the inevitable question. 'Tell me, Emma dear, just what are you planning to do once you've finished your schooling?'

Julian looked up at the older man, 'I'm thinking of taking up acting as a profession. Enrol at RADA...'

'Tosh!' came Charles's sharp reply. 'What you should consider is becoming a writer. That sketch you wrote for my houseguests to perform was quite, quite brilliant. Forget acting, that's a profession for inflated egos with no personalities of their own, hence they have to be given one. You have a brilliant mind, you're funny and I can see you simply pouring out tomes in the line of dear old Willy Maugham and even that wonderful Saki. The writer, not the delicious libation!' He looked across at the stunned Julian. 'Come here and live with me, my dear boy and start to write!' Leaning forward conspiratorially, Charles added sotto voce, 'I know all about your stepfather by reputation. A total shit and bastard from what I hear and, worse, much worse, a vicious out-spoken homophobe.' Leaning back in the comfortable poolside chaise, he added, 'You've just turned sixteen so when you get back, face the music and tell him you will have nothing more to do with him! You won't need any money – you'll be here ostensibly as my secretary and will be on a more than adequate salary.' The shrewd eyes looked at the stunned young man with an even stronger intensity. 'Will you miss your mother?'

'My mother,' responded Julian, not missing a beat, 'is a vapid, stupid bird-brained bitch! Who else would have demeaned herself to sink so low as to have married such a pig and, what's even worse, allow him to frenziedly fuck her and enjoy it?' Lowering his eyes and, at the same time fluttering his glitter-enhanced eyelashes, the teenager murmured coquettishly, 'Thank you, Auntie Carlotta, I have great delight in accepting the even greater honour of being your new secretary.'

'Good,' smiled Charles. 'And now we've sorted that little problem out, let me put my final hand of cards on the table. Ah Massivestuffa. Like some glorious, gigantic, priapic genie you always appear when needed. Emma and I have just fluttered bracelets on the deal I discussed with you after that rather delicious session of arabics last night.' He gave the beaming Moroccan a sly wink, adding with a giggle. 'I'm surprised dear Emma here hasn't notice his old auntie sitting very side saddle this merry morn! But, enough about my holy of holies. I think a bottle of the merry Widow will not go amiss and, along with her glorious, golden showering, a dash of fresh peach juice, *vouz ne pensez pas*?'

Giving a nod of his massive head, the smiling giant left in a rippling of bronze muscles.

'My cards on the table,' repeated Charles. 'Dear Dougie – until you came into my life, Julian Emma Bovary – was the most important persona, ever, for me. Everything I have goes to Dougie. You haven't seen my home in Tangier – known as Hutton's Hump! – for even that embittered, hung up – with hung being the operative word – old bitch was said to have been jealous of the Villa Cerne Abbas , named not after it's owner but after the giant of Cerne Abbas, a naked 55 metre high figure carved into the chalk hillside of the village of the same name. The Abbas giant boasts not only a massive penis and even more terrifying club so, instead of a typical, dreary English name for an ex pat's home – for example – Mon Repos – I thought why not go for something a bit more er…in keeping with the locals I have met?' Charles paused before taken a deep breath. 'However, I've been speaking to Dougie about what I am about to say and he is, I must assure you, one hundred and ten per cent in agreement. Both he and I adore your company, you've brought even more sunshine into this sunshiney haven and that is why I have happily offered you a permanent job here. But it doesn't end there. I really want you to live with me, him, us, wherever that may be. When I die – no, please don't interrupt, Emma dear – when I die, a third of my estate will come to you. What do you say?'

'What do I say?' muttered a stunned Julian, adjusting his feather boa (with Charles, no matter whatever the dress for the morning, boas were de rigueur at breakfast). He paused for a moment to regain his usual now regal composure. 'Jesus, Charles…'

'Aunt Carlotta, per-lease!'

'Aunt Carlotta… I'm completely overwhelmed. Shocked, excited – in fact if you have a Roget's Thesaurus I'll happily spend the next few weeks marking the relevant adjectives!'

'Spoken like a true writer! So I can take it that somewhere amongst all those adjectives will be the two words I'm most anxious to hear? "I accept."'

'I accept!'

Charles's wicked, gnome-like face broke into a delighted smile.

'But with one exception.'

'And that is?' From Julian's expression the old roué' simply knew that the exception would not be an unpleasant one.

'On numerous occasions I have come out with Flaubert's quote regarding my doppelgänger, namely, Madame Bovary, c'est moi! However, may I assure you, this Madame Bovary will never, ever, indulge herself to drink her predecessor's favourite – and final – tipple of arsenic!'

'Why a mere tipple when you'd be able to purchase a laboratory or two or even a hundred and three!' chuckled Charles, adding hastily, 'a joke, Emma! A joke! I'd much prefer seeing you buying up Messrs Tiffany, Boucheron and more!'

A LONDON CLUB – SEVERAL YEARS LATER :

'Whatever happened to that stepson of yours? That milksop? Julian, wasn't it?'

'God, David! And to think I was just beginning to enjoy myself!'

'That bad, is it?'

'No, not bad at all, if you distance yourself from it. The little sod finished his schooling and then, without so much as a by your leave, went off to work – and here I use that word in its every context – for some richer-than-Croesus old homosexual in bloody Tangier of all places. Broke his mother's heart.'

'How is the magical Mrs M?' cut in David Maloney, somewhat concerned by the darkening, purplish hue of his companion's face.

'Magical?' John Masterton gave out a derisive snort. 'More the maudlin, fucking miserable, menopausal Mrs M!' He took a large gulp of his whisky soda before beckoning a waiter for two refills. 'You were right as bloody usual, David, when you gave me your personal view on life, "Make no purchases and you buy no pain." No, no... that's not quite right, something more to the effect of 'If it flies...'

'If it flies, floats or fucks, rent it!'

'Too true! Too true!' John Masterton gave a hollow laugh. 'You know, David, at first I really loved her and indulged her with all her fantasies. I never went so far as to buy a plane but the stint with that yacht, Daphne 2, was a disaster! And now, what with all those hot flushes and mood swings as she approaches fifty, it's mood swings, tears and more tears and, let me tell you my friend, you can forget the fucking!'

'So, there is something very rotten in the present State of Masterton?'

'Rotten? That's putting it bloody mildly! Even cancerous is too mild a word! Thank Christ she's taken herself off to stay with some friend in Cheltenham for a few days. At least I won't have to sneak into the bog to have a wank in the morning!'

David gave a smile and pointed to their almost empty glasses. 'Drink up, my friend. What you seriously need is a bit of divertissement, maybe even a bit of the old hank panky! Do you remember the Jamiesons?'

'You mean Maudie and Hamish, I take it? Yes, of course I remember them, Great fun couple. Why?'

'They're holding a cocktail party this evening.' David glanced down at his gold Piaget watch. 'It's not that late, in fact, things should only be starting to hot up around now. Why don't we call by there and then I'll take you out to dinner somewhere salubrious!'

'Where's the party?'

'Eaton Square, but no problem, I've got my car and driver outside.' David couldn't resist a laugh. 'Both rented!'

'James! What a lovely surprise!' A smiling Maudie Jamieson proffered a smooth, surgically enhanced cheek for the large, bluff man to kiss. 'I was hoping David would twist your arm into coming. So much more fun than the two of you sitting drinking in that stuffy club of yours!' The petite, blonde, exquisitely groomed and coiffured woman gave his beefy arm a squeeze. 'And how is the delightful Daphne?'

'Oh, just too, too delightful, Maudie. Just too, too deliriously delightful… A laugh every long drawn out minute!'

'Oh!' exclaimed Maudie Jamieson, slightly taken aback by the cynical reply. She looked around the large, airy drawing room in a slight panic. 'Oh look! Elizabeth Bartholomew has just walked in! I simply must go and say hello!'

'Humph!' said James, reaching for another glass of champagne from a passing tray-bearing waiter. He surveyed the elegant, laughing, well-groomed, attractive guests moodily. 'So, if it flies, floats or fucks, rent it, huh? Well, why bloody well not? Maybe David and self can hit a club later and see what's available.' Gazing disparagingly around at the animated crowd he suddenly found himself riveted by a stunning brunette clad in a an equally stunning bright red cocktail dress and a pair of the sexiest, high heeled red, strappy sandals. The young woman appeared to be deep in conversation with a man James vaguely knew. 'Obviously not in the rent stakes,' James muttered to himself, his spirits rising for the first time that evening, 'but an old ram can dream, can't he?'

Making his way over to the couple he patted the tall, grey haired man heartily on the back. 'Tony, old thing! How the devil are you? Long time no see!' he bellowed, while giving the startled brunette a broad wink. 'Trust Tony Walker to find the most attractive woman in the room!' Switching on his most ingratiating, shark-like smile he held out beefy, manicured hand. 'James. James Masterton and you are…?'

'Oh, allow me!' cut in Tony Walker, a small look of irritation on his smooth, wax-like forehead. 'My house guest, Elida Cabaca from South America. Rio to be exact.'

'Ah yes, Rio!' said James expansively, reaching for another drink from a passing waiter. 'Rio the city of Sugar Loaf, the Copacabana, Ipanema…er Corcovado'

'Yes,' smiled Elida Cabaca icily, her annoyance at the bluff man's rudeness apparent. 'That Rio!'

An embarrassing silence settled upon the three.

'Yes. Exactly. That one.' said James in a lame attempt to break the growing tension.

'Do you know Rio, apart from the names?' The brunette's voice was both husky and seductive but unrelenting.

Christ, thought James. We've got a real ball breaker here! To his amazement he found the sharpness and the closeness of the svelte, elegant woman causing a stirring in his heavy penis, a waft of her musky scent seemingly to excite and titillate his olfactory senses and further stimulating his now semi-erect, thickset organ.

'I have to confess I've never been to Rio,' said James, looking sheepish. 'But I have seen your lovely city numerous times in films and on TV!'

'Not quite the same thing,' said Elida Cabaca, a small teasing smile playing on her full, luscious lips. To the relief of the two men she added huskily, 'Maybe the two of you will come and pay us a proper visit sometime?'

'Us?' This from James.

'My partner and I.' She looked up quizzically at the now beaming James whose erection was making a superhuman attempt to burst out of its restraining Calvin Kleins. 'Did you say Masterton?'

'I did indeed,' smiled James, moving his large, muscular legs uncomfortably. Bloody cock! 'James Masterton, at your service Senorita Cabaca.'

'Well now there's a coincidence. My partner's name is also Masterton, Julian Masterton. Maybe the two of you are distantly related?'

'Julian Masterton? Did you say Julian Masterton?' James's bushy eyebrows had shot up in disbelief. 'I had a stepson – I mean I have a stepson named Julian – he took my name as a child.' The big man shook his silver leonine head in disbelief. 'No,' he gave a derisive laugh. 'Your partner couldn't be our Julian.' James let out a relieved chuckle. 'This Julian Masterton lives part-time in the South of France or Tangiers, or did, the last time we heard of him.'

Elida gave a warm, throaty laugh, showing a perfect set of dazzling white teeth. 'That's exactly where we met. Julian used to share a villa there with another Englishman a Douglas Hawkins. The two of them are in business with my brother in South America. Douglas handles the European side and Julian advises my brother with the Latin American side, hence the two of us spending a great deal of our time in Rio.'

'Good God!' James's heavy jaw literally dropped with astonishment. 'Julian advises your brother in business?'

'Quite, quite brilliantly! Alvar – that's my brother – says he couldn't run the business without Julian's help. It's a family business and, until Julian came along and waved his magic wand, we were really in dire, dire trouble.'

'Well I'll be damned!' blustered James. 'Well I never!'

'But isn't this the most incredible coincidence?' cried Elida, clapping her long, elegant hands together, her large brown eyes shining with excitement. 'Tony! Tony! Why don't the three of us have dinner… Oh!' she looked up the now decidedly uncomfortable but beaming man (James could feel the slimy tumescence leaking from his now throbbing erection). 'How rude of me, perhaps you have a prior engagement?' Elida gave a mischievous smile. 'I'd love to hear more about Julian. He's always been most mysterious about his past and then here, out of the blue, I meet his stepfather!'

'Well, if you're sure…'

'Of course I'm sure! After all, it's not everyday one meets a member of ones' missing family!'

'I did actually come here with an associate.'

'Oh, invite him as well! You can be my Three Musketeers!'

'What?'David gave a glance in the direction of the couple now talking animatedly. 'She's a looker alright, a bloody stunner! But what the fuck's she doing staying with that old pouf Walker?'

'Pouf or no pouf, 'James leaned forward to whisper stagily into David's ear, 'the stunning house guest is my pansy son-in-law's partner, would you believe?'

'My dear James, in this day and age I'm prepared to believe anything!'

Dinner concluded, David excused himself while Tony too began making his excuses to leave.

'Would you care for a nightcap at Annabel's' offered James suddenly, mentally willing Tony to say no and Elida to say yes.

'Not for me,' said Tony, giving Elida a knowing glance. 'You two go on and enjoy yourselves.' The tall man stood up before bending over and giving Elida a kiss on the cheek. 'You have your key, darling and, if you're not too late, I'll see you at breakfast.' Giving James an airy wave Tony wended his way out of the crowded restaurant.

The time at Annabel's, the prestigious, private Mayfair nightclub, passed – for James – in a daze of mounting excitement. My Calvin Kleins are well and truly fucked, he thought laughingly to himself, as he pressed his blatantly erect penis closely against Elida's hot crotch and erotically undulating body as they made their way around the small, dark, crowded dance floor to the motivating sounds of the seductive music.

'My, my,' laughed Elida softly, her warm breath caressing James's ear, who, due to his vast height, had his head slumped down against the young woman's shoulder. She gave a further undulation of her warm mound. 'Naughty, naughty monster James! Like stepfather, like stepson!

'Elida, Elida,' croaked James, his throat dry. 'Would you…?'

'Like to come back for yet another nightcap? You wicked, wicked macho man you!' Elida gave a light laugh before nipping him teasingly on his large, fleshy earlobe. 'And why not?' she added softly. 'I take it your wife's away or are you suggesting a hotel?'

'Oh no, no hotel. Thank God for this night of coincidences. She's away!'

Satiated after a night of rampant, almost unbelievable sex, James lay drowsily against the silent figure lying next to him, his large, hairy fingers gently stroking the still damp and sticky, dark hairs of her pubic mound. 'I think I'm falling in love with you,' he muttered softly to the quietly dozing figure. Not expecting any response he slyly slid his thick forefinger into the tender, warm, depth of her slit, pushing the monster finger in right up to the knuckle.

He heard Elida give a sharp intake of breath.

'It's not just the sex we've just had, which was, for me, the best ever, but it's you Elida. You're all woman.' James gave a soft laugh as he inserted a second finger, his penis stirring once again as he felt her raise her receptive cunt in response. 'A blonde is no match for a brunette, no matter what they say!' Giving a deep sigh Elida gently removed James's fingers from inside herself and lifted her lithe frame up onto one elbow where she lay looking at him, her eyes unsmiling, her dark hair tumbling around her elegant shoulders.

On noticing the young woman's dull, almost catatonic gaze, James gave a nervous smile. 'Does Julian realise how lucky he is?' he asked tentatively.

'Oh yes, he most certainly does!' Elida gave a dark, hollow laugh. Still lying on her side, her head and shoulders supported by her right arm, she continued in a haunting, low sing song voice. 'They do say, stepdaddy dear, revenge is a dish best served cold, but, in your blighted case, a dish served hot, cunt hot. So, say good morning stepdaddy dear to your stepdaughter Elida alias, your stepson Julian! Yes James, you've just fucked and fucked again, me, Julian, or Julia if it makes you feel even more disgusted! But look on the bright side, at least you didn't have to fuck me up the arse!'

On seeing the growing horror on James's face, the now wild-eyed woman gave a triumphant shriek. 'Yes James, I had a sex operation in South America some years ago. Brunette like that eternally fucked secretary of yours, Noreen Butterworth, never fails to appeal, does it? Blonde to brunette was easy. Blue eyes to brown? Contact lenses. And by the way, in comparison to Doug, my husband, lover, partner et al, sex with you is how I imagine it must be if you're into bestiality and prefer rutting with a pig!'

Giving a light, satisfying, triumphant cry, Elida sprang from the large, rumpled bed. 'You've been set up James Masterton, and don't you ever forget it! And now, if you'll excuse me, I'm out of here. As they say in Rio, adios you cancerous old bastard!'

James Masteron, business man supreme, began to scream. He was still screaming several hours later when the police, along with an ambulance, arrived having been called by the housekeeper. The elderly woman, on hearing the animal-like screams and howling when returning from her weekly, early morning visit to the various markets, duly accompanied by her butler husband had found their employer rolling naked on the fouled bedroom carpet, screaming and eating his own excrement.

Today James Masterton resides in a private clinic, Since that fateful morning he has not uttered a single sound apart from the occasional, demented shriek.

ANOTHER NOTCH
IN THEIR BELT

Soups's three greatest pleasures were to sniff, suck or slurp! Sniff because nothing was quite as invigorating as a good healthy inhalation of a good stink up the nostrils – the more pungent and malodorous the better! Suck because it was only then you managed to draw out the flavour and the more you salivated on the object of your desire the more tantalising the taste! And as for slurp – could there ever be a comparison to that bold licking, the tonguing and the... well, slurping? The more saliva, the more the compelling of the transference of that compelling flavour from it's hot, foetid surface into one's own mouth – the ultimate of hedonistic satisfaction.

Not everyone took to Soups and his indulgences. Marie was always complaining – she objected most strongly at the wetness of his slurping and as for his breath? Forget it (even though this wasn't always possible!).

'I don't know how you can allow him to do that to you!' she would complain to David as she watched her lover fondle Soups as the third of their ménage greedily slurped industriously at some exposed part of David's receptive anatomy. 'It's disgusting!'

'Well, I don't mind him doing this all over me at all!' would be David's laughing and far from pacifying response. 'You ought to be grateful he's sometimes into girls as well! And let's face it, once he gets going on you, you never say no! Make no bones about it, Soups always goes for the male crotch as opposed to the old camel hoof – you being the exception!'

'Don't be so revolting!' Marie would shriek with unfettered delight. 'Between the two of you it's more than a simple girl should be allowed to endure!'

'Aw, come on, Marie. You know you love it. What with me fucking you and Snoops taking care of the other, you're in – if you'll excuse the double entendre – doggie heaven!'

'I find it ungainly on all fours!'

'Yeah, but you love it!'

Soups, the third of this torrid triangle would sit panting, his long pink tongue occasionally flicking upwards and around his wet mouth, watching and listening to the friendly sparring between his two greatest friends. How he loved them! How he loved those incredible intimacies they shared!

The only game he wasn't completely happy with – and one David seemed to enjoy with extra relish – was being forced into wearing a heavy collar attached to a leash. Playing master and slave however, was not an option if the other three indulgences were to take place.

Clandestine meetings did occur and loyalty could be stretched. Soups, for all his devotion to David and Marie had an uncontrollable lusting for Dennis, a handsome neighbour who, when the two were able to get together (it took some devious sneaking about) would indulge in a wild, delicious, rumbustious, no-holds-barred romp!

Oh, the pungent aroma of Dennis's cutely crinkled sphincter! The taste of those fit-to-burst cheeky balls! And while Dennis wasn't too keen on being mounted – after all it wasn't natural according to him! – he never said no to an energetic dry humping.

And so it went blissfully on. The occasional, illicit indulgences with the always willing Dennis and the guaranteed threesomes involving David and the not-always-so-pliant Marie. But, as they so truthfully say, all good things come to an end. And this it did, and all because of – well, as you may have guessed – a female!

Soups's reaction was as if he'd been hit by a speeding truck. One moment it was a case of guaranteed daily bliss with David and Marie along with the alternate dalliances with Dennis where – and only with Dennis – there had been several unsuccessful attempts at a type of buggery (Dennis was not prepared to play preferring wild, wet snuffling rimming and ball licking instead) and then, KA POW!

Her name was Mitzi.

While Mitzi had been living only a few houses away, unlike Soups the young lady was the plaything of a rather strange young man named

Freddie. Although Freddie appeared to be gay it was obvious he adored Mitzi and she appeared to be the sole benefit of all his indulgences and ostentatious wealth. According to David, Freddie 'had inherited' and was 'a fucking faggot' but to Soups, Freddie's devotion to Mitzi surely must have proven that he played in both camps or – to use another expression he'd heard – was 'bi.'

Until that fateful day Soups had paid little or no attention to the sprightly Mitzi. Of course he had seen her sitting aloof alongside the uptight, pampered Freddie as they drove past in Freddie's equally pampered silver BMW convertible (how could a car look so clean?) but, up until this moment, it had been the olfactory delights of his two friends and Dennis which had satisfied his innermost desires.

Mitzi changed all that.

In a mere few seconds Soups had sensed an odour the power, the intensity and the allure of which he had never experienced before. Forget David and all his personal indulgences; forget bum teasing Dennis; Soups was obsessed. There was no alternative, he simply had to fuck her.

As if aware of Soups's intentions Mitzi seemed to have gone into hiding but whether out of view she was not out of mind and come what may, Soups was determined to complete his quest. His chance came one early evening while David and Marie were having a quiet drink on the patio. Soups, without even excusing himself had made his way sneakily over to Freddie's pristine house where – he could instinctively sense it – Mitzi was alone on their patio. Stealthily approaching the screened-off area (he'd even gone so far as to sneak through a neighbour's hedge!) Soups could sniff, smell and almost taste the object of his desire. A strange feeling was taking place in his groin, a feeling which could only be remedied by one aggressive act. With an alien snarl Soups shot onto the patio and before the startled Mitzi could react, he was on top of her, his long, organ gleaming like a lethal, highly polished pink projectile.

His victim didn't have a chance. With a loud yelp she found herself suddenly penetrated with a vicious, painful thrust. With a further yelp she was mounted vigorously from behind and then the fucking began! How Soups pounded away, piston-like, on the yelping, yowling Mitzi. It was nothing more than rape, a glorious uninhibited day light rape! Forget any former sniffing, sucking or licking! This was it! This was the real McCoy. Soups's orgasm (his first) surpassed anything he had ever experienced. Having shuddered and jettisoned his load into the now quivering but passive Mitzi, he quickly withdrew and without as much as a by-your-leave, slunk off back through the hedge from whence he'd come!

Nine weeks later to the very day of the rape, a proud Mitzi gave birth to a litter of five healthy puppies. It took only a few weeks for the still furious Freddie – after all, it was his precious baby who had been so viciously 'interfered with' (Freddie would never have used the work 'fucked') – to work out who the culprit was.

Meanwhile, his guilt had led to an almost delicious mental self-flagellation! If he hadn't so carelessly left Mitzi for those few moments on the patio while on the phone to his boyfriend Charles the dirty deed would never, ever have taken place. He would have simply 'shooed' the dreadful intruder away!

He was later even more deliciously chastised by Charles who – in between laughing cruelly at Freddie's choice of such a butch action (shoo) – could not quite come to grips at his boyfriend not realising his precious baby was on heat and oblivious to the fact 'every fucking mongrel on the fucking block would have a go given half the fucking chance!' As he sarcastically pointed out, for a dog 'It's just another notch in their belt!'

Mitzi, instead of being in disgrace, found herself the over-indulged, much-worshipped martyr! Sweets and more treats helped her through her pampered pregnancy and Freddie was proud to announce that 'within minutes' she had regained her former figure.

However, what he did find a 'bitter pill to swallow' was the fact that precious baby, being a petit, miniature poodle, had had to go and lose her virginity to a Bassett Hound.

THE PICTURE OF DORIAN GAY

The spacious studio, an ugly extension protruding into the overrun garden of the equally neglected large Victorian red brick house, was considered by the neighbouring residents in the quiet, residential Chelsea street, as both a mystery and also an eyesore.

'A disgrace and letdown to the neighbourhood' was the almost daily mantra of the formidable Mrs Jennifer Rutherford, a former councillor and ardent troublemaker.

'And that ivy!' Enid de Fable, her companion, an equally formidable woman of similar years would constantly exclaim. 'Why, all the windows facing the street are positively blinkered! The owner can hardly get any daylight at all!

The owner, or so rumour had it, was a wealthy, retired antiques dealer (who, unbeknown to his neighbours had been the discreet winner of a lottery rollover involving several millions) whose hobbies (again only known through hearsay) included both painting and ornithology. With the latter he had developed a firm interest in taxidermy (he had once gone so far as to donate a stuffed seagull to the local Conservative fete!). The ex-dealer lived in nigh-on seclusion, an enigma to his neighbours, his only noticeable forays being regular visits to his local where again he remained a usually solitary figure. On some occasions he would be joined by another male companion, his guests always young and ordinary enough in looks so as not to be given more than a cursory glance by the other customers.

'Right weirdo, he is,' Dick, the publican was fond of saying to the drinkers sitting at the bar, nodding in the direction of the departing figure after one of these typical visits. However, on this particular evening he was proving to be more verbose than usual. 'Always has a bottle of champagne, that Veuve Clicquot, very posh! Insisted I got a case in specially and paid me in advance!' Warming to his subject, the portly man continued. Tapping his large, red nose knowingly he, he added sotto voce to his now rapt audience, 'Always sits in what I call the Black Hole – the darkest corner of the bar. Used to own a shop in the Pimlico road but sold it some years ago, or so I've been told. Must have come into some money 'cause he bought the Lander house but seems to have done nothing since.' Pulling another pint for one of the avid listeners, he couldn't help adding darkly, 'Lovely house it was but he seems to have just let it go to rack and ruin.'

'Dick's right,' chipped in Molly, his chirpy wife and co-manager. 'Maudie, Maudie Collins who does for Mr Dorian – that's his name – says that apart from spending most of his time in what he now calls his studio or workshop but which was the old ballroom; he only uses the kitchen, study and a bedroom bathroom on the second floor; nothing else. In fact Maudie tells me that the rest of the rooms, some twenty in all, remain empty!'

'Very odd,' agreed old Phil, another regular. 'All them rooms empty, you say?'

'All,' said Molly nodding her blonde head emphatically. 'All twenty of them. And,' she added, leaning forward confidentially, 'Maudie tells me that although he only occupies those few rooms, he insists on keeping the whole house heated, winter and summer! Imagine the cost of that!'

'What a waste,' commented Daisy Drew, another regular known as 'Down the Hatch, Daisy!' 'As Phil said, it used to be such a lovely house when the Landers owned it. Why, I believe it even had a ballroom!'

'That's what I've just told you,' said Molly irritably. Daisy, after her third gin tended to become a tad tiresome. 'He now uses the old ballroom as a studio and workshop. Maudie tells me it's quite strange what he gets up to, stuffing animals and only painting the faces of young men.'

'Stuffing? Paintings? Young men?' Phil, a lewd smirk on his face couldn't resist the obvious, 'What do you mean by stuffing animals?'

'Not what you mean, you dirty old bugger!' laughed Molly. 'He's one of them taxi whatsits.'

'And the rest,' sniggered Phil. 'Young men's faces? You got to be joking!'

'He's a taxidermist,' cut in Dick ignoring Phil's innuendos. 'They stuff dead things. Birds and such.'

'Well, I only stuff birds!' grinned Phil with another dirty snigger.

'And we don't need to hear such talk in here, thank you!' said Daisy primly in between giving a discreet hiccup.

Molly, always one to keep the peace, said to no one in particular and much to Phil's delight. 'Mind like sewer, our Phil.'

'A blocked sewer,' chortled the leering old man.

'Voices down!' hissed Dick, slamming down a glass heavily on the bar top. 'He's just walked in.'

Dorian Montagu, the subject under discussion, stood quietly by the entrance door eyeing the small group seated at the bar counter. Standing half hidden by his tall frame was the shadowy figure of a young man. Having directed his companion to the aforesaid darkened corner table, Dorian confidently made his way over the bar. 'A bottle of my usual, please Dick.' He semi-whispered in a smooth, silky baritone.

'As always, Mr Dorian,' smiled the publican. He nodded towards the now seated figure in the shadows. 'I'll bring it right over and, as I see you are not alone, I'll bring two glasses.'

'Thank you,' whispered the tall, thin, cadaverous-looking figure. 'And if the fair Molly could organise us two of her delicious toasted ham and cheese sandwiches, that would be most admirable.' With a thin smile Dorian turned and made his way back to the corner table.

'Christ! He looks exactly like that Christopher Lee character,' muttered Phil. 'Perhaps he sucks the blood from those young lads he brings in here – or something else!' he chortled. Seeing Molly's frown of disapproval he added lamely, 'Like that Dracula fella he always plays…'

'Oh, don't be ridiculous, Phil!' scolded Molly playfully while deliberately choosing to ignore the elderly man's sly jibe. 'Mr Dorian's quite harmless.' She gave a giggle. 'What he really enjoys are munching on my toasted cheese sandwiches.'

Had Phil been about to come out with another lewd comment he thought better of it and remained silent.

'So, you're a visitor to London.' A statement, not a question. Dorian raised his wine glass filled with sparkling liquid. 'Well, welcome visitor!'

'It's Tony,' said the young man defensively. 'I told you that when we met.'

'I know it's Tony, Tony!' smiled Dorian, showing a perfect set of gleaming white teeth. 'Tony Burton, in fact. And I'm…?'

'Dorian,' said Tony, now relaxing. He gave the tall, dark haired, middle-aged man a tentative smile. 'Dorian Montagu.'

'Well done,' smiled Dorian. 'So, Tony Burton, now I've dragged you away from the rather dubious surroundings of the Queen's Head, what else are you planning to do while visiting our fair city?'

'Oh, the usual touristy things. Visit a few galleries; take in a few shows. See the Changing of the Guard...'

'And you're staying where?' said Dorian, cutting in, his face impassive, while thinking, A possible number twenty though a rather mediocre one! Why do all pretty young men, whether locals, tourists or whatever – especially those gay – have to be so predictable and so camp? He turned his attention back to what the young man was saying about staying in some hotel in Earl's Court. 'And how did you know about the Queen's Head?' he asked, interrupting once again.

'Oh, it's in my gay guide to London.' Tony gave a dismissive shrug of his thin shoulders. 'However, there doesn't seem to be much going on in Earl's Court. I'm told most of the action happens in Soho and a around a place called Vauxhall. But the Queen's Head was a start.' He looked up at the contemplative Dorian, a grin appearing on his smooth, lightly tanned oval-shaped face. 'Where I just so happened to bump into you,' he added with a slight, camp giggle.

'Were you attracted to me?' asked Dorian, bluntly, giving a slight wince at the young man's almost effeminate laughter.

Tony gave a startled jerk of his head, the blond hair flopping down over an eyebrow. 'Well, er...yes! You looked – you look – like a nice guy and when you had a drink sent over to me I thought it only polite to come over and say thanks.'

'I'm glad you did,' smiled Dorian. 'Most young men simply accept the drink and give me a nod. So, thank you again, I appreciated the gesture.' He gave the young man another contemplative look. 'And when I asked you if you would care to join me for a bite to eat?'

'Oh, I was quite prepared for you to ask me out!' The young man's smile was now both open and suggestive. 'Back in Cape Town – that's where I'm from – I'm always being asked out!'

"South Africa? I thought I detected a slight accent.' Dorian gave another thin smile. 'You don't look very South African!'

'Not all South Africans are big, butch, rugger buggers!' giggled the young man again. 'There are a few more er... shall we say, civilised sorts like myself.'

'Quite,' agreed Dorian, a touch sardonically, 'And are you travelling with someone?'

'No, I'm travelling alone.'

'That's very adventurous.'

'But I am adventurous,' camped the young man, his smile broadening.

'Good.' said Dorian.

'Your sandwiches.' said Molly.

'Watch this,' said Dick knowingly. 'They'll finish the bottle – maybe even have a second as there are two of them – and then Mr Dorian will order two large Courvoisier bandies. After that they'll leave. I'll bet on my last penny he'll more than likely take the young man back to the house!'

'Well, it's none of our business!' retorted Molly, somewhat loftily. 'Live and let live is what I say and I don't need to hear your opinion on that, thank you Phil!'

Dorian led the way along the quiet street towards the tall, dark, brooding house. During the short walk he kept making discreet sidelong glances at his young companion who appeared more interested in the tall, imposing houses they were passing than in paying any attention to his host. Perfect, Dorian was thinking to himself, perfect. A slender bender and – if all his former skinny lookalikes are anything to go by – with luck, one with a monstrous member! Dorian stopped in front of a tall, black painted wrought iron set of gates. 'We're here,' he said in his low, quiet voice. 'Watch your step as the paving stones can be a bit treacherous.'

'Is this whole place yours?' Tony looked slowly around the massive, shadowy entrance hall, his eyes having gradually become accustomed to the gloom, settling on a grand staircase rising majestically ahead of them and disappearing up into the shadows of the upper floors.

'Yes, I bought it about ten years ago.' Dorian gave a hollow laugh which echoed eerily around them. 'Before moving in I did have the grandiose idea of redecorating the whole place but after a day or two in residence, I simply decided let things stay as they were and have never gotten round to changing anything. I live mainly in my study and my bedroom on the second floor. The remainder of the house remains exactly as it was when I moved in. Empty!' He looked at the puzzled face in front of him. 'Don't be too alarmed, young Tony. There's a thoroughly workable kitchen with all mod cons – as with all the bathrooms – plus an extremely well stocked wine cellar!' Dorian then gave a small, twisted smile. 'But then, of course, my pièce de résistance…'

'Piss de…?'

'No Tony, pièce de résistance!' Dorian gave a light laugh. 'No piss about it at all! It means the most important or remarkable item.'

'Sorry, Dorian.' Tony gave a camp smile. 'You must think me one of those dizzy blonds!'

'No, not at all!' replied Dorian, thinking, No, not a dizzy blond, dearest. Simply a fucking ignorant one! 'My pièce de résistance is my studio and workshop.'

'Studio? Workshop? You're an artist then?'

'Well, let's say an amateur artist. It's one of my hobbies.'

'One of them?'

'Yes. I have two major hobbies. Painting and taxidermy.'

'Taxidermy?'

'I stuff dead things. Birds mainly and at times the odd small animal such as a fox or a badger.'

'Yes!' said Tony excitedly, 'Like you see in the museums!'

'Yes,' said Dorian dryly. 'Like you see in museums.' He gave a flash of teeth, bright white in the gloom. Now, how about that drink I offered you? More champagne?'

'That would be great! Thanks.'

'Follow me through to the kitchen. This way, left of the staircase.'

Busying himself getting a pair of flutes from the extensive, oak panelled run of cupboards along one side of the vast room, Dorian gave a quick glance over his shoulder at Tony who was now examining a series of stuffed birds sitting on one of the kitchen counters.

'Christ, you almost expect them to suddenly flap their wings and fly!' he laughed.

'That would be too Alfred Hitchcock!' laughed Dorian. 'Though, come to think of it you do look rather like Miss Tippi Hedren!'

'Alfred Hitchcock? Tippi Hedren? You've lost me, I'm afraid,' giggled Tony.

'Quite,' muttered Dorian. He set the two flutes down on the large central kitchen table and began opening a bottle of champagne he'd taken from a large double-fronted fridge. 'Were those sandwiches at the pub sufficient for you or would you like something else? A pizza perhaps? I can easily put one in the microwave.'

'A pizza? A pizza would be great!' exclaimed Tony. 'I must say, I am still feeling slightly peckish!'

'As I said,' said Dorian smiling. 'Very Tippi Hedren. Very The Birds.' Jesus, change that from dizzy blond to bird brain!

Tony remained looking nonplussed.

'Old Alfred joke, forget it!' smiled Dorian. 'One pizza coming up!'

'And after we've had our pizza, may I see your studio?' The young man's voice was eager.

'I thought you'd never ask!' laughed his host, reaching in to fetch a large frozen pizza from the freezer.

The studio workroom, once the ballroom extension to the house, caused Tony to stand, literally open mouthed with amazement. 'Why, it's massive, Dor!' he gasped.

Dor? Dorian gave a shudder. 'Yes, isn't it!' he agreed, the sarcasm in his voice going unnoticed.

'But…' Tony gestured at a solitary easel sitting in the centre of the cavernous space. 'I don't see any paintings?' Peering more intently into the gloom he pointed excitedly towards a long workbench set against one of the high walls. 'But I can see some more stuffed birds. And, wow! Is that a dog?'

'Yes. He's called Rufus – or what used to be Rufus. He was a Labrador I used to own. He died of old age and I thought it would be quite fun to keep him around. He was a great friend.'

'May I take a closer look at Rufus?'

'By all means.' They walked slowly over towards the silent dog standing in front of a set of high French-style windows leading onto the dark garden. Tony laid a tentative hand on the animal's soft, furry head. 'He doesn't look very old,' he observed, peering at the silent, glass eyes staring spookily ahead. 'In fact, he looks extremely fit and healthy!' The young man gave a slightly nervous laugh. 'I can only say, Dor, if you hadn't told me he was stuffed I could have sworn he was alive and about to lick my hand at any moment!'

'Oh, he's stuffed, alright.' Dorian assured him in his smooth, soft, silky voice.

Tony turned back again to the solitary easel, eyeing the shrouded canvas resting upon it. 'What are you working on at the moment?' he asked, pointing.

'A portrait.'

'A portrait?' Tony's eyes widened. 'What of?'

'A person, Tony. Portraits are usually of people and sometimes animals, usually of the face but sometimes the whole figure. Here, have a look.' Dorian stepped over to the easel and, using both his long arms pulled the cover away from the canvas in one sweeping movement.

Tony stood staring blankly. 'It's a bloke!'

'Yes Tony, a bloke or, as I prefer to call him, a young man. And before you ask, yes, and I only paint young men. Have a look.'

Dorian moved swiftly across the shadowy room to a nearby wall containing a metal plate bristling with light switches. With a quick movement of his fingers he flicked several of these resulting in a battery of spotlights flooding the cavernous room in a dazzling glare of bright, white light.

'Christ!' cried Tony, momentarily blinded and shielding his eyes from the unexpected brightness. 'Christ!' he said again, his eyes now adjusting to the sudden change. Hanging on the high windowless wall facing the opposite wall of French-style windows were row upon row of portraits, each of a young man staring glassily ahead, some dark haired but the majority blond and all in their late teens or early twenties. 'There must be at least twenty or maybe even thirty.' He whispered.

'Twenty four, to be exact,' said Dorian crisply. 'The one I'm currently working on will be the twenty fifth.' He pointed to a double sized empty space in the uppermost row. 'After I've finished with this one, I'll have one more to do.' Looking at the fascinated young man he muttered, in almost inaudibly, 'And why not you?'

'Pardon? Said the young man.

'I was about to explain the centre portrait which, as you can see is a full sized painting of a blond young man sitting upright in a chair.' What Dorian did not go on to elaborate was the fact the young man was nude with his lithe, muscular legs spread wide apart, his heavily veined, uncircumcised penis hanging sloth-like between the smooth thighs. 'That's Ben,' whispered Dorian. 'He was my first model and the only young man I've ever painted as a full figure. All the rest are just faces.'

'And you know all these blokes er... guys? And do you still see them?'

'I knew them all,' replied Dorian silkily. 'I knew them all well.'

'Knew them?' Tony gave another puzzled look. 'Don't you see them anymore? Any of them?'

'All these questions, Tony!' laughed Dorian dismissively. 'And yes, in answer to your question. I don't see them anymore, nor need to see them anymore as I have their portraits to remind of how they all were at their best.'

Tony, about to ask the further, obvious question as to why at least one out of the twenty five young men hadn't remained a friend or at least kept in touch, decided – on seeing Dorian's tight lipped expression – best not to.

'Time for another brandy before we retire,' said Dorian firmly, moving back to the switches and starting to flick off the lights. 'I take it you're planning on staying the night, Tony?' Seeing a flicker of hesitation in the young man's eyes, he added less brusquely. 'Unless you would prefer me to order you a taxi to take you back to Earl's Court? It'll be charged to my account of course.'

After a moment's silence Tony gave a warm, almost coquettish smile. 'I'd really like to stay.' He gave a camp giggle. 'Who knows, I may even end up portrait number twenty six and, better still, remain a friend!'

'Many a word spoken in jest,' smiled Dorian.

'You mean you'd like to paint me?' Tony's already high pitched voice reached an even higher decibel level.

'Why not?' said Dorian. 'That's if you're not too busy visiting galleries and searching for other gay venues over the next few days…'

'All that can wait!' said Tony, his eyes widening. 'Wow, imagine me in a portrait! Wait until I tell the people back home!'

'Your family?'

'No, I've got no family.' Tony's face took on a suitable sombre expression. 'I live with an elderly aunt but, as she's not too fond of her strange nephew, I spend more time at my college.'

'Many friends there?'

'Not really. I'm a bit of a loner.' The young man gave a soft sigh. 'I spend most of my time reading. I plan to be a writer one day, another Dan Brown perhaps!'

'Well, good luck to you. Now, how about that brandy?' We'll take that in the study.'

And why not another brandy and maybe a few more days here as the resident model? Tony was thinking. At first I found you a bit creepy Mr D but the more I listen to you the more I see you as a bit of a harmless, eccentric old queen! You're obviously loaded so why not stick around if you're going to show me a good time?

Having followed Dorian through into the warm, book lined room he sat himself down comfortably onto a large wingback chair as directed by his host. A gas log fire burned brightly in the highly burnished grate, this and one large table lamp being the only illumination inside the high ceilinged study. 'You've certainly got a lot of books,' said Tony peering at the seemingly endless shelves. 'Have you actually read them all?'

'Yes,' answered Dorian handing him a generously filled brandy balloon before settling himself in a large, matching chair opposite. 'In fact,' he said, putting his glass down on the mahogany butler's tray table separating them, 'Before I went out and before I had the good fortune of bumping into you, I was just rereading an old favourite of mine.' Leaning forward Dorian picked up a leather bound book lying on the table. 'It's titled The Picture of Dorian Gray. Do you know it?'

'By that old queen Oscar Wilde, isn't it?'

'Yes,' said Dorian, slightly irritated by Tony's lack of respect for one of his favourite icons. 'As you so subtly put it, by that old queen, Oscar Wilde.'

'Something about a picture in an attic, isn't it? A picture that shows all this bloke Dorian's faults. Hey, Dorian!' he announced, his light, clipped South African accent becoming more pronounced with his growing excitement at the way the evening was turning out. 'You've got the same name as the character in the story!' He let out a high pitched giggle, the combination of the warm room, the champagne and brandy now definitely taking its toll. Attempting to stifle a further set of giggles, he managed to splutter out, 'Don't tell me Dor that you too have a portrait of yourself stuck away in some attic in this vast old house?'

'No, not of myself,' said Dorian, a small, faintly sinister smile again playing on his thin lips. 'Someone else.'

Tony stopped in the middle of another burst of the giggles. 'You're joking me?' he said, his voice faltering.

'No, I never joke when it comes to my work,' said Dorian giving another tight, even more sinister smile. 'They say seeing is believing. Care to see it?'

'You bet!' Tony took a deep swallow of brandy before allowing himself a small nervous laugh. 'Kind of spooky though, you know, what with your name being Dorian like the character in the book and now you telling me you have an attic with a painting in it!'

'Oh, it's spooky alright! Come along. Let me get you a refill and bring your drink with you. You may need it!'

Taking the proffered brandy balloon Dorian returned to the open bar cupboard and silently poured the refills. With a quick sleight of hand he took two small white tablets from a pill box resting on the serving shelf and dropped these into Tony's glass. 'Follow me.' he said, handing over the glass with its generous helping of the rich, amber liquid.

Dutifully the young man took his position behind his host as Dorian led the way across the vast tiled hall to the wide staircase. Treading carefully up the highly waxed, dimly lit bare steps they reached the first landing where Dorian flicked a second switch lighting up the next flight. Tony, to his astonishment, noticed a single hanging naked bulb as the only form of illumination. Large, dark, intricately panelled wooden doors faced silently onto the landing with its bare, highly polished wooden floor and devoid of all furniture or paintings.

'The next floor contains my bedroom, bathroom and a dressing room,' announced Dorian. 'After that we have two more floors to go before the final staircase to the attic.'

They proceeded to climb slowly, Dorian's leather soles making a sharp clacking sound as opposed to the slight squeak of Tony's trainers.

'Almost there,' Dorian confirmed in a strangely spectral-like echo caused by the empty void surrounding them. 'And here we are!' He pointed to a final, sharply rising, narrow staircase leading up to another closed door. He looked at Tony who by now had broken into a slight sweat and breathing heavily. 'You alright?'

'Fine, a bit hot but I'm also feeling a bit strange…a bit hot and a bit dizzy…' The young man's eyes began to swivel in panic.

'Must be all the drink,' laughed Dorian. 'And yes, it is hot. Although the house is basically empty I do keep all the heating on come rain or shine. Hold on and try and make the next flight. There's the odd chair or two in the attic so you'll be able to sit down. I can also get you a glass of water.' He held out a thin, long bony hand. 'Let me help you.'

Leading the young man cautiously up the final flight they entered the dark room softly lit by the dim reflection of a street lamp outside. 'Here, sit down on this chair and I'll get you that drink.'

'Thanks,' muttered Tony, sinking gratefully onto the upright, wooden chair. He held out a shaking hand to take the glass from Dorian. Draining this in a few gulps he wiped his mouth with the back of his hand before looking up at Dorian, the look of panic returning to his face. 'Christ, Dorian! I think I'm about to pass out…'

'But not before you've seen the portrait,' demanded Dorian. 'And here it is!' He added dramatically flicking on a battery of ceiling spots.

Tony, his eyes blurring and his head spinning, squinted blindly towards where Dorian was pointing. 'But,' he said, his voice slurring, 'I can't see any painting.' Screwing up his eyes once more he managed to say, 'It looks more like a model, a seated figure. He blinked again, leaning forward in the chair. 'It is a model.' Tony gave a drooling gasp. 'It's that friend of yours in the full size portrait in your studio!'

'Well done, Tony,' smiled Dorian, taking the glass from the relaxing fingers. 'It is, in fact, the real Ben. I literally stuffed him after I'd finished the painting.' This he added quite calmly and quietly. Taking a firm hold of the young man who was desperately trying to raise himself from the chair, he lifted him effortlessly in his strong arms, dragging him over to the silent, seated figure. 'And what else do you see?' The question was asked with a malicious snarl. 'What else do you see, Tony Burton? Tell me what else you see?'

A vigorous shaking of his swaying frame resulted in Tony's head clearing for a brief moment. He peered in a horrified fascination at the long, irregular tubular length running down from between the figure's parted legs, ending up in a pink coiled heap between his bare feet. 'Looks like a bloody string of joined up sausages instead of his cock,' Tony managed to gasp and despite his dizziness and nausea, he couldn't resist a snigger.

'In a way they are,' said Dorian proudly. 'You're looking at a string of stuffed cocks, all of which belonged to the boys whose portraits you saw downstairs. Ben was the only young man I kept intact. The rest, once I had painted their heads were all – apart from their cocks – incinerated!' He looked at the now horrified young man. 'Twenty four cocks in all, Tony. Just under three metres of deliciously coiled cock and you, young man, are about to become the twenty sixth portrait and the final cock!'

BITE SIZE

'I hear Jazzy Jeremy was up to his tired old party trick again last night! A repeat of last week's dinner, this time at Jay Metcalfe's. Apparently Duncan Meredew was not amused!'

'When was Duncan Meredew ever amused? Come to think of it, what on earth induced Jay to ever invite Mother Meredew?'

'It was a last minute resort. You know how precise Jay is about his placement! I must say I'd rather have odd numbers as opposed to a moronic make do!'

'Let's face it sweetheart, with Duncan Meredew as a guest, equal numbers or not, you would have still ended up with an odd number. According to Johnny G the whole evening was such a disaster that even the soufflé decided to collapse!'

'Miss Jay's face must have been a picture.'

'Well, I wouldn't go so far as to say quite that...'

'Can you hold on a sec? My other phone...'

'I'll call you back in five. I'm desperate for a pee, anyway!'

'Charming.'

'Hi, me again. I've had an idea. Why don't you and I hold a small dinner week after next? We can give it in the private room at Ronaldo's.'

'As long as you pick up the tab, sweetie! Not all of us are inheritance queens!'

'That goes without saying apart from "thank you Aunt Dora!" But listen, here's the pièce de résistance. We give the dinner for Jeremy!'

'Jeremy Craggs? Jarring Jer? The Grande Hoover Dame? Tell me you're joking?

No, I'm deadly serious and listen before you sneer! There's method in my madness. Here's what I'm planning, no, make that what we're going to do!'

A stunned silence followed the brief description of the dinner-to-be, 'You still there?'

'Of course I'm still here! Just stunned into silence by the genius of it all! Do think it could really work?'

'Trust me Bobs. Simply put your faith into your old chum Giles. So, are we on?'

'You bet!'

'Right, get out the old diary and let's make a tentative date. First I'll check if Pat's free and we'll take it from there. If Pat is available, I'll ring Ronaldo's and book the room. Hey, you free for lunch?'

'Could be.'

'Scalini's at one? I fancy a bit of pasta!'

'So that's the name of the waiter you fancy?'

'Bitch!'

'See you at one.'

TEN DAYS LATER:

'Buono sera, Signor Taylor, Senor Maddox! All is ready for you. Two of your guests have already arrived. Antonio is your barman for the evening and your favourite waiters Gustavo and Marco will be looking after you during dinner. Buon appetito!'

'Than you, Mario' Giving the beaming maître d' a warm smile, Giles, followed by an equally smiling Bobs, walked through to a small, second reception area at the rear of the busy restaurant and into the private dining room and bar.

Tony Graham, a short, stocky dark-haired stockbroker gave his host an affectionate hug before standing back and looking admiringly at the tall, blond, handsome young man, casually elegant in a Gieves and Hawkes blazer, striped open neck shirt from Turnbull & Asser and a pair of bright red corduroy trousers.

'And Bobs! Like two peas in a pod apart from the pants!' (Bobs was wearing a pair of emerald green cords).

'Such a way with words,' smiled Giles, giving Johnny, the other guest, a mischievous grin. 'I must remember to use that phrase again some time. Two peas in a pod, huh? Hopefully that was just a minor slip of the tongue and you meant to say two penises!

'I…' Tony gave a confused look and then broke into a knowing grin. 'Well, yes. If that's what you'd prefer!'

'We'd better be!' said Bobs, cutting in. 'Two penises, that is. And with you and Johnny, that makes four!' He gave a small chuckle. 'Jazzy Jeremy has also been invited, if you catch my drift.'

'Oh shit!'

'And before you decide to scarper, Johnny, it get's even worse. I've told the Jer that the dinner is for him…'

'Double shit!'

'And here's the reason why.'

Having given a brief résumé regarding the reason for Jeremy's inclusion for the dinner, Giles ended by saying, 'Although the others are not in it, as if it were, nobody will be the least surprised as our dear Jeremy's reputation certainly precedes him.'

'Fucking brilliant!' laughed Tony.

'I'll drink to that!' cried Johnny.

'Pat! You made it!' This from a delighted – and relieved – Giles.

'Not even that fucking volcanic cloud would have stopped me!' laughed the big genial giant who had just joined the group. 'On hearing the Iceland irritation – that bloody volcano – was about to cause another bout of flight chaos, I took the precaution of returning from Salzburg a day earlier on Euro Star.'

'Quite right,' agreed Charles, another new arrival who had just walked in accompanied by two other guests, David and Gus. In a few moments the party of eight were standing around in the small bar area, drinking and chatting amicably.

'And here's James,' said Bobs with a grin as a tousled, red-haired young man entered the now crowded space. Having greeted the latest arrival with a hug and a kiss and making sure he was offered a drink, Bobs turned again to Giles. 'And where do you think our guest of dishonour has gotten to?'

'Obviously the jarring one is hoovering it up in the Plough a few doors away and just waiting to make an entrance. And speaking of the she-devil...'

'Am I late for my very own dinner party?' At the sound of the high pitched camp falsetto heads swivelled and a silence descend on the group. 'Tell me I'm not!' The voice carolled again. 'I could have sworn the delicious Giles said nine and yet here you all are, gloriously groomed, gloriously grouped and gorgeously gorgeous!'

'Pity he didn't say nein!' said one of the group just loud enough for those nearest to him to overhear.

'My, oh my!' shrieked the unabashed young man. 'New faces! Well, hello faces old and new. My name's Jeremy and isn't my party going to be such fun!' A statement, not a question. Jeremy held out a limp, thin hand to the sober-suited Charles who was looking suitably taken aback by the pencil thin, bleached headed figure standing in a balletic pose in front of him. 'And you are?' The question was asked with a pursing of his cupid bow-like lips and a fluttering of darkened lashes. (As Giles was to say later to Bobs, 'I could have sworn he was just about to do an entrechat right into poor old Charles's arms!').

'Er...Charles,' said Charles gruffly. 'Charles Donaldson.' He took the limp, proffered hand in his large, hairy one. 'And this is David...'

'Oh, lordy, lordy! So many names! I'll simply have to call you all darling and have done with it!' Accepting a flute of champagne Jeremy's eyes widened as he noticed the tall, bulky, suited figure of Pat who was eyeing him with some amusement.

'And whom may you be, kind sir or' – and here Jeremy couldn't resist a further shriek – 'should that be Big Sur?'

'Pat,' said Pat, unfazed and eyes twinkling. 'But Big Sur will be fine!'

Jeremy looked up coquettishly at the rugged, now smiling face towering above above him. 'And Big Sur you shall be!' he squeaked.

'Shall we go into dinner?' suggested Giles.

As the guests gathered around their host, Giles, pointing at the round table, continued. 'Pat, I'm putting you over there. Charles you're there.' Having seated an excited, still shrieking Jeremy between Charles and Gus, he then placed the remainder of the guests accordingly. As Marco duly filled the wine glasses with a crisp, dry Sancerre and the starter course was being served, Giles turned to Johnny seated on his right. 'Christ, Mistress Jer was pissed when she arrived and the rate she's going I only hope she doesn't let us down with her usual cabaret spot!'

'Don't worry,' said Johnny, reassuringly. 'Miss Jer usually disappears in the middle of the pudding and getting thoroughly pissed is par for the course.'

The dinner progressed smoothly apart from the never-ending hysterical shrieks coming from the guest of honour. With the two handsome waiters deftly serving the delicious, prearranged menu and the vigilant Marco ensuring the glasses were never empty, the main course was eventually finished and the plates cleared away. It was then Giles gave Bobs a knowing wink, Jeremy – as anticipated – had slipped silently from his chair and was now, literally 'under the table' and obscured from view by the long tablecloth.

The first reaction came from Charles who gave a sudden start and then started talking animatedly to Gus across the now empty chair between them. After a few minutes the big man burst into a sudden fit of coughing. David, sitting on Charles's right, was next to give a grunt before taking a large gulp of wine.

'Always anti-clockwise,' whispered Giles to a giggling Johnny.

'No wonder he's so damn skinny,' Johnny managed to comment. 'No calories in the pudding he's swallowing!'

'I'm next,' warned Giles, 'and then it's your turn followed by Bobs's. Then Pat, or, as our friend has dubbed our genial giant, Big Sur!' The latter being said with a slight grunt as Jeremy, happily performing his party piece, energetically began blowing his host.

It was a foregone conclusion that whenever Jeremy came to dinner, all the guests came too! For several years he had scandalised – and thrilled – gay dinner parties by sliding down under every available table and going around on his hands and knees, unzipping the guests' flies, and swallowing his 'pudding' course with a gluttonous delight. On all occasions some of the guests had been forewarned while for others, the after dinner treat came as a complete shock or pleasant surprise. Having 'done the rounds' Jeremy would re-emerge on to his seat and continue drinking and chatting as if he had never been absent.

'One to go,' smiled Giles, giving a grinning Bobs another wink.

The piercing shriek came a few minutes later followed by an enormous crash which saw the whole table being lifted into the air causing glasses, crockery and cutlery to go flying.

'You bastards!' shrieked a hysterical Jeremy, clawing his way frantically from between the deep folds of the tablecloth. Emerging both dishevelled and wild-eyed, his face puce with fury, he stood shaking uncontrollably amidst the laughing diners. Pointing an erratic arm he glared at his exultant host. 'You cunt!' he screeched.

'Not him, darling!' guffawed Pat, eye's streaming with tears of laughter. 'Me! You've obviously never gone down on a diesel dyke before!'

PIED PIPER

Ernest Craig suffered two major problems, himself and his doppelgänger, the niggling, nagging Ernest B.

Ernest A simply loathed his alter ego, Ernest B; the strange sibling rivalry remaining in an almost constant state of flux.

'Fuck you, Ernest B!' Ernest A would say in frustration when shaving to the similarly lathered Ernest B, reflected in the shaving mirror.

'Up yours, you pathetic arsehole!' or something equally flattering would be the inevitable response from the inverted Ernest B, more often than not followed by an expletive 'Shit! There was no need to nick me, you bumbling cunt!'

However, when it came to making up Ernest A and Ernest B enjoyed nothing more than a sweaty, groaning, mutual wank!

'Thank you,' Ernest A would say to Ernest B as they lay together, Ernest A looking down at his still twitching, long, thick cum-covered cock.

'No, thank you,' Ernest B would drowsily respond, 'Only next time, not so rough please.'

This strange, volatile combination of Ego and Id lived together in a dank, claustrophobic, rundown cottage known as The Rookery, set on the outskirts of a small isolated village named Hadlington in northern Yorkshire. Had it not been for the presence of an ugly, granite Victorian church, the mediocre containment of a mere fifteen families would have been known as a hamlet.

'The last drop of a piss shake on the floor,' Ernest A would repeatedly quote to 'that silly old codger,' the querulous Dick Dennis, known to the locals as Bull's Eye Bill in honour of his continued skills at the de rigueur darts' sessions in the Green Shepherd each Friday evening. The almost daily exchange of so-called witty repartee would take place in the aforesaid Green Shepherd, Hadlington's only public house, where Ernest A would slide onto his bar stool precisely at seven minutes past noon, never earlier and never later. As always, Ernest A's favourite tipple, a sickly mix of sweet Cyprus sherry and vodka, awaited him. Ernest B strongly disapproved of 'the dreaded drink.'

'It'll make you impotent if you are not careful' he would continually admonish an inwardly sulking Ernest A as they lay in their narrow bed at night. 'And you know what that means, more cock-a-doodle-don't than cock-a-doodle do!'

'I'll show you what my cock can doodle do!' would be the guaranteed retort. 'And as my cock is your cock, so you cock-a-doodle-do it too!'

As the locals fondly observed the plodding, slow Ernest A, little did they realise they were also in the company of Ernest B. Ernest A's continual expression of puzzlement – he would be conversing mentally with Ernest B – when having one of his mumbled, limited conversations with a fellow inhabitant, caused many sympathetic murmurings such as 'short of a couple of pence' or, as the bitchy Caroline St John – Hadlington's answer (or so she thought) to Paris Hilton – put it, 'The token village idiot.'

Apart from his routine act with Bull-eye Bill, Ernest A kept much to himself. His mother, the long-suffering Silvia Craig, had been abandoned by her husband (or so her story went) soon after Ernest's birth. The woman had appeared off the local bus, literally, almost a Dickensian character with the child in her arms and a single, battered suitcase by her side. Added to the mystery of the mute woman was a letter from the former owner of the cottage saying the property now belonged to the new arrival. Having made enquiries as to the whereabouts of The Rookery, Silvia Craig had simply made her way along the dirt road leading from the village towards the woods and to where the cottage lay near to an evil-looking piece of marshland.

From that day her return visits to Hadlington had never varied. Once a week she would receive an envelope with a London postmark and once a week she would return to the original bus stop of her arrival, catch the bus on its way to the larger neighbouring market town of Moorsfield and return the same day laden down with several shopping bags. Not once, in the whole time of her living at The Rookery did she ever shop or socialise within the village itself and soon after her arrival, even the solitary, weekly letter had stopped.

It was almost as if the young lad, like his mother, had also suddenly materialised. One day a bulky six year old had presented himself to the local school teacher and handed over a note from his mother. The message in the neat handwriting was succinct, Dear Miss Codlington, I have pleasure in introducing my son Ernest for you to inspire, groom and teach. Thanking you. Yours sincerely, Mrs Silvia Craig.

To say that the incident was, without a doubt, the most sensational event to occur in the sleepy hamlet that year would have been the equivalent of saying Her Majesty was an adulteress!

'You could have knocked me over with a feather!' Miss Codlington, the bird-like school teacher never tired of chirruping. 'There he was – ever so neat I must say – but with this sad and worried expression on his pale almost old little face and with his mother's note. An educated hand, by the way, and ever so polite. How the woman knew my name I'll never know! Why, I swear you could have knocked me over with a feather!'

The bulky, expressionless and sullen Ernest was duly placed at a desk where he would sit for the next few years absorbing the meagre offerings of learning doled out by the constantly frustrated Miss Codlington. On being asked to answer a question the boy would never speak but would insist on writing his reply. He was never incorrect.

'I think,' Miss Codlington had confessed to the Reverend Porter one night at the Bingo after a sherry or two too many, 'We may have a genius here. Ernest never speaks – oh, don't get me wrong, he's not a mute! – Ernest has a very sweet speaking voice, if a bit slow – but I can tell he's always deep in thought. He thinks a lot. Hence my private name for him – I have private names for all my pupils – Rodin!

'Rodin?

'After his statue of The Thinker, if you see what I mean!'

On the few occasions the Reverend had witnessed the bumbling boy around the village he had to confess to himself that he could see no connection with The Thinker at all.

Having been confronted by the determined – 'I will not take no for an answer!' – Miss Coldlington, Ernest was duly cajoled by the teacher into joining the small school band. The ensemble, comprising of a drummer, a pianist and a guitarist saw the young boy blossom into a fairly accomplished trumpeter.

'While he may appear morose and sullen most of the time he seems to positively blossom when playing the trumpet!' the sherry-inspired Miss Codlington had confided to the benevolent Reverend Porter on more than one occasion. 'I would almost go so far as to say he lives through his instrument!' was another much repeated confidence.

'From thinker to trumpeter, eh? Quite an about turn if I may say,' mused the man, his sarcasm overlooked by the beaming Miss Codlington as she held out her glass for a refill from a passing parishioner acting as waitress.

Ernest had drifted away from his great seat of learning and began taking on odd jobs on local farms and around the village itself. It had finally occurred to the now ageing Reverend to one day approach the by now massive young man and ask him the burning question. 'And how is your mother, Ernest?' (Mrs Craig had not been seen catching her usual bus for some length of time with Ernest carrying out the weekly routine himself).

'Gone back to London,' had been the mumbled reply and that was that.

Caroline, who held the exalted position of barmaid at the Green Shepherd, could always be guaranteed to let out a parakeet-like screech at her so-called wit. The buxom blonde would also let it be known that Ernest A was 'One of those still waiting to come out of the cabinet!' Such riveting news was widely accepted by the likes of Ted, the publican, the aforementioned Bull's Eye Bill and several other regulars who would gather in the evening to refresh themselves on cheap tipples and gossip.

Caroline's bald, beefy but otherwise extremely hirsute partner, Reg, the proud owner of the local garage, slogan – 'Let Reg Repair You!' – had let it be known that he had met 'them sort before' when doing his apprenticeship in nearby York. 'Special pub there for them lot,' he would say to his agog audience. 'Full of them fucking – pardon my French, Cal – fudge packers! Me and me mate, Bert, having dropped in there for a drink one evening by accident – Bert's even a bigger bugger than me (Reg was apparently unaware of this slip of the tongue) – but I tell you, the two of us got the fuck – pardon my French again, Cal – out of there before you could shout shirt lifter!'

In tight-lipped agreement with Caroline and Reg was Miss Harriet Hanson, an embittered spinster of some fifty plus who owned the one and only village shop which also served as the local post office.

'Filthy one of those,' she would confide to Doris Bridlington-Smythe, wife of the local MP and therefore considered by some of the villagers as minor royalty. Doris B-S had never 'let on' that Peter B-S had made his money through a series of dodgy building deals during their earlier years 'down south.' Making a subtle exit from 'The City,' the couple had reinvented themselves, the purchase of The Manor, the local 'big house,' being the final icing on Peter B-S's corrupt cake.

'Who said you can't have your cake and eat it?' the large bluff, man would loudly claim. When more inebriated – which was often – he would confide to the likes of a giggling Caroline (Doris allowed him the occasional foray to the Green Shepherd as it makes his constituents aware that he was 'one of them.') 'And I can certainly tell you, young Caroline, back in my youth I wasn't known as Pete the Meat for nothing, if you catch my drift...'

Caroline, whose mantra among many was 'seeing is believing' had been given the opportunity one evening after Reg had been called out to deal with a breakdown on the nearby motorway and Peter was making one of his 'I'm one of you' visits to the pub.

Slightly the worse for wear – he had consumed several double whiskies – Peter had slyly come up with his pseudonym once more and suggested he and Caroline go 'somewhere private' so the giggling blonde could judge for herself. Not only had the young woman let out a startled squawk on seeing Pete's treat (she had later confided to Flo from the Co-op that it made Reg's prick look like 'a pinkie finger' in comparison to Mr Bridlington-Smythe's mighty 'python!').

'I tell you Flo,' she had said to her equally giggling friend. 'I came over all faint I did, at the size of it!'

'Silly cow!' cried Flo, shrieking with mirth. 'I would have dropped to my knees and thanked God for big mercies!'

'I was taught never to talk with my mouth full!' screeched an almost hysterical Caroline, once again quite overcome by her own wit.

Apparently unaware of her husband's indiscretions, Doris Bridlington-Smythe was acutely (or so she thought) aware of the indiscretions involving others.

'My husband and I' or the more plebeian 'Petah and I' were her favourite introductions to any salacious follow on. After Harriet Hanson's snide comments regarding the bumbling, sullen Ernest, Doris – having given a discreet (and modest) tiny cough from behind her bony hand – added her Petah's own damning indictment by concluding with the words '... and forgive me for using such a word but – to quote Petah further – "such perverts should be..." oh, excuse me if I spell it out, c-a-s-t-r-a-t-e-d!'

'Oh?' Remembering her own personal traumas when Worzel, her pet tom had been 'doctored' it was Harriet Hanson's turn to give a discreet, embarrassed cough. The thought of Ernest losing his 'danglies' was almost too much to comprehend. However, as her best friend Doris B-S was the wife of an MP no less, she had no alternative but to nod her neat, grey-permed head in vehement agreement.

Taunting and snide remarks were not limited to a few vicious grownups. As with most children considered 'different,' Ernest had been systematically teased and bullied by his school mates and later on, with the mantle of village idiot pressing heavily upon his wide, stooped shoulders, he continued to be the butt of jibes, asides and jokes.

With a stoic, sullen indifference, Ernest appeared to ignore the insults and in doing so became more and more of a recluse. His only appearances in the village occurred when doing some part-time work at the school for the always loyal Miss Codlington.

It went without saying that along with the bigots the most vindictive of all were the children. Cries of Shrek! or even the totally unwarranted and mystifying paedophile! were but a few of the taunts left hanging in the air albeit whilst working around the school or occasionally cutting the grass on the village green and in the church yard (two further tasks instigated by the loyal Miss Codlington).

'I don't know why you put up with it, Ernest A,' Ernest B would say after a particularly hurtful barrage of abuse. 'That young Dennis Carter needs a punch in the mouth, if you ask me!'

'Did I ask you, Ernest B?' Ernest A would respond.

'No, but I feel the pain as much as you do, Ernest A. And,' here there was a knowing chuckle, 'I also know what you're thinking!'

'Exactly, Ernest B, so why pursue it? All in good time, all in good time.'

If only they'd given him the chance, the likes of Caroline, Reg, Ted, Bulls-eye Bill et al would have found that their so-called village idiot was, in fact, a highly intelligent man who did nothing to alleviate the general opinion of himself. Unfortunately – as the offensive villagers were to eventually discover – this intelligence rode hand in hand with a deeply hidden and very disturbed, violent streak.

'Morning luv!'

Caroline looked up at the two men who had just entered the pub. Both smacked of the word 'worldly-wise' and the other word, perhaps even more magical, 'press.' (She had been quick to notice one was carrying an expensive-looking camera).

'Morning, may I help you?'

'Hopefully you can. We're trying to find one of your residents, a Mr Ernest Craig.'

'Ernest Craig?' Caroline's eyes widened. Why on earth would anyone want to find Ernest? She gave the two a quizzical look. 'Yes, I know Ernest, he's a regular.' Changing immediately into her gossipy, barmaid mode, she eagerly continued. 'In every day like a well-oiled clock for his usual tipple – but a loner, a real loner is our Ernest.' She tapped her bleached head with the end of a long red fingernail. 'Not quite the brightest bunny in the hutch, if you catch my drift.' Noting the obvious interest of her audience she changed tactics and, eyes narrowing shrewdly she brusquely asked, 'Why? What's he done?'

'More of a case of what's he won!'

'Won?'

'Yes, luv. Won.' The man minus the camera leant forward conspiratorially. 'We've managed to get here before the others but you'll more than likely be swamped in the next day or two!'

'Others? Swamped? Won? What ya going on about? What's Ernest Craig gone and done? Murdered his mum after all?'

'No, miss. Ernest Craig is no murderer – not to our knowledge – but he is a lottery winner. The latest jackpot, a bloody whopping eighteen million quid!'

'Fuck!' said the Paris Hilton lookalike. 'Fuck!' she said again before shakily pouring herself a large brandy and simply handing over the bottle and two schooners to the two men. 'Jesus,' said Caroline. 'Jesus fucking Christ! Tell me all about it. Meanwhile, swallow those while I get my bag. I'll take you over to his cottage.' She gave what she considered her most dazzling HELLO Magazine smile. 'Dear Ernie is a great friend of mine and I'm sure he'll be only too delighted to have a picture taken of him and me for your paper when I make the introduction!' She gave them another of her beady looks. 'He doesn't know?'

By this time a still stunned Caroline had gathered up her handbag and was now about to make her way to the main door. Not waiting for a response to her question, she continued grimly. 'I certainly would have known if he'd had a letter or received a message. Harriet Hanson the post mistress would have told me. Ernest doesn't have a phone and occasionally has been known to make a call from her shop. The only person to receive any mail in that family, ever, was his ma and that stopped soon after her arrival. Ernest makes a weekly trip to Moorsfield so he must have a collection point there.'

The sharp-looking man, minus the camera, gave a tight smile. 'Letter or no letter, he knows alright, luv! In fact, on learning of his win he was, at first, planning to remain anonymous but then he called my editor at the Moorsfield Mail last week and suggested we came down and meet up with him today. We've been given exclusivity for his story and, to quote Ernest, "I wish my dear friends in Hadlington to be the first to know! The general media can then pick it up from there!"'

Caroline arched a severely plucked eyebrow. 'The win has obviously loosened his tongue, then! The guy's never been known to speak more that a few words and then those are mostly grunts!'

By this stage the three were walking briskly side by side up the lane towards The Rookery with Caroline, her mind in a complete state of flux, completely ignoring the cheerful acknowledgements of a few locals whose smiles turned to sudden, curious stares at the sight of their usually friendly barmaid deep in determined conversation with the two shifty-looking strangers. The additional viewing of what could only have been an expensive camera case had also caused a ripple of intrigue.

The two men stood alongside the young woman looking at the derelict, overgrown, crumbling cottage, in disbelief.

'Someone actually lives here?' questioned the one who, by now had introduced himself as Tim.

'What a shit heap!' observed the one with the camera who had subsequently introduced himself as Geoff.

'Well, let's see what he has to say, shall we?' said Tim, smiling thinly. Turning from the two he tapped briskly on the shabby front door.

After a few moments the front door was duly opened.

'Ernest?' Caroline's jaw literally dropped at the Ernest lookalike standing, smiling in front of her. Gone was the sullen expression; gone was the lank, unkempt hair; gone were the shabby clothes. Instead, there stood this smiling man, his hair neatly trimmed and styled and, in lieu of his usual baggy sweat shirt and jeans the new Ernest was wearing a neat open-necked blue and white check shirt, navy double-breasted blazer, neatly pressed rust-coloured chinos and a pair of gleaming Gucci loafers! Unknown to Caroline and her two escorts they were now in the presence of Ernest as his Super Ego, the blending of the former Ernest A (Ego) and Ernest B (Id).

'Caroline! And a very good morning to you!' The voice and the face were the same but the smile (in fact, as Caroline was to remark later to an agog group in the pub, she had never seen Ernest smile before) along with the general makeover was almost too much for the young woman who visibly took a step back in shock.

'Ernest?' she managed to gasp for a second time.

'Yes, Caroline. Ernest.' The still smiling man ('he must have had one of them whitening jobs!' was another of Caroline's later observations) proffered a large, beautifully manicured hand to an equally amazed Tim, The Gentleman's Quarterly vision in front of him being totally alien to his surroundings. 'I take it you two gentlemen are from the Moorsfield Mail?'

Tim, having released the genial giant's hand looked again at the still bewildered Caroline. 'May we come in?'

'Please do.' said the still smiling Ernest. 'My home isn't much but – like its owner – it's also about to have a complete makeover.'

To Caroline's even further surprise (could there be any more?) their genial host offered them a flute of champagne each. 'I did some necessary shopping in Moorsfield last week,' he explained as he deftly poured the (chilled) sparkling liquid. 'Bought some proper champagne flutes to go with this Dom Perignom – not like the wine glasses you use for your so-called champagne – that Prosecco – in the pub, Caroline!' – the young woman visibly flinching at the jibe. – 'I brought all this stuff with me when I came back late last night along with a few more new clothes…'

'On the bus?' queried Caroline.

'No Caroline, not on the bus; in a hire car with a driver.' Still smiling he raised his drink. 'Cheers!' He pointed to the two chairs and the sagging, shabby, stained sofa. 'Please sit down.' Giving a soft chuckle, he added. 'Tomorrow I have a top interior designer coming up from London especially to see me. Once we've met and agreed his designs, the transformation of The Rookery will begin.'

'You're going to be staying here?' Caroline's question came out in a shocked squeak.

'But of course,' came the smooth, soft reply. 'Like Hadlington, this cottage is my home, the only home I have ever known! I was brought here as a child and here I plan to stay.'

'But…but…' stammered the young woman.

'But what, Caroline?' said Ernest, but this time in an even more soft and silkier tone.

'All that money!' she blurted out.

'Exactly!' smiled the lottery winner. 'All that money.' He took another sip of his champagne, relishing the looks of the usually venomous but now utterly deflated barmaid. 'But, back to business and the reason why you're all here! I take it Caroline you are not only here to congratulate me but also to appear in a photograph alongside the lucky winner in tomorrow's paper!' (A statement, not a question). Ernest gave Geoff a wink, adding 'You'll be syndicating your photograph, I take it? All those London papers will no doubt be gagging for a copy!' This time it was Caroline's turn to receive a wink. 'You're about to become an overnight celebrity, Caroline! My, oh my! Imagine all that jealousy and envy should they think you're the girl friend of a multi-millionaire?'

After a series of photographs had been taken (Geoff was to later say when back at the paper's offices, 'Thank Christ for airbrushing! At least I can obliterate all that shitty background shit!) and the two men, along with the still stunned Caroline had left, Ernest A turned to Ernest B (on these intimate occasions Super Ego tactfully withdrew).

'What do you think?'

'Brilliant! Ernest A! That Caroline cunt is going to take some time to get over the shock of Super Ego when he takes over. I think, however, the greatest shock was the new articulate you. She looked as if you'd suddenly gone from speaking English to Swahili! She's never heard you mumble more than a few words in the pub!.

'From mumbo to jumbo!' quipped Ernest A.

'Oh Ernest A, at times you positively slay me!' chortled his other half. 'I know I'm always criticising you and your penchant for the demon drink but what about another bottle of that delicious Dom Perignom?'

'You're on, Ernest B, and as you are being so charming, may I suggest – as a savoury course – a long, slow, pissed mutual wank?'

'Why, wank you Ernest A! Just what I was about to suggest myself!'

Back at the Green Shepherd a preening Caroline sat holding centre stage. ''Eighteen million!' She kept saying. 'And if you still can't believe it, just wait until you see the picture of me and Ernest in tomorrow's Moorsfield Mail!'

'Why are you in the picture?' demanded Harriet Hanson somewhat spitefully.

'Why not?' said Caroline. 'After all, everyone in here has known Ernest virtually all his life which makes us all his friends so I don't see it as any sort of favouritism in any way!'

'Oh, but of course.' said a tight-lipped Harriet, for once put firmly in her place.

The incredulousness at Ernest's decision to keep the cottage was almost as much as that at the news of his massive win.

'If it was me, I'd buy myself something like The Manor where the Bridlington-Smythes live. If not even bigger.' This from Ted, the publican.

'I'd buy myself one of them Bentley jobs…' mused Dick, aka Bull's Eye Bill, 'and a Jag for the missus!'

'I'd take a world cruise,' said Harriet Hanson firmly, little knowing how fortuitous for another this comment would be.

While the group fantasized over what they would have done had it been one of them and not Ernest winning the breathtaking prize, it all kept coming back to Caroline's endlessly repeated observation. 'But it's the way he spoke! He never stopped! Just went on and on using them posh words like that guy on the telly, that David Dimbleby! Very la di da di bloody da!' Remembering her reputation as a wit she quickly added, 'Like that bloody frog turning into a prince!'

'Did you kiss him then, Cal?' asked Reg with a mischievous grin.

'For eighteen million quid I'd do more than bloody kiss him!' The beaming barmaid gave a shriek. 'I tell you something, young Reg; you've got an awful lot of proving to do to make sure that me sticking around you is worth me while!'

'I'll stick to you later!' came the guffawed reply.

SPRING – THE FOLLOWING YEAR:

Whereas Harriet Hanson would never go on her luxury cruise, Miss Codlington did. To Harriet's chagrin – and the rest of the group – the gentle school teacher had been treated to a three month luxury world cruise plus a gold American Express card to be permanently taken care of by Ernest's London accountants. However, the crème de la crème was an immediate one hundred thousand pounds deposited into her small savings account by her devoted 'Rodin.' Miss Codlington, still unable to grasp her immense good fortune, took – on Ernest's insistence – an early retirement and it was a smiling Ernest himself who personally saw her set sail from Southampton in the uttermost of luxury. Apart from several postcards from exotic locations, the elderly school teacher seemed to have disappeared. After a time a final transfer of all her new funds banked in Moordfield was discreetly made to a sister branch abroad.

Meanwhile The Rookery, its derelict appearance a thing of the past, had, according to Tim of the Moorsfield Mail, now been transformed from 'a modest cosy cottage into a Petit Trianon; a veritable Les Petit Versailles!' As promised by Ernest, he had been given full exclusivity with the Ernest Craig story.

Caroline, to her heady delight, had been dubbed by a decidedly tongue-in-cheek Tim as 'Hadlington's Marie Antoinette,' the sobriquet coming after she had been photographed several times – on Ernest's insistence – along with the smiling, immaculately groomed multi-millionaire owner both inside and outside the building as more and more remarkable changes were taking place.

'I tell you Tim, that guy's up to something! And it stinks!' Geoff would repeatedly comment after another visit to The Rookery to capture the changes in progress. (The two had been summonsed by Ernest who, in the meantime, was temporarily living in considerable style at the Moorsfield

Holiday Inn during the extensive refurbishment to the cottage while still a regular visitor to the ever changing site).

'And all those two-faced villagers he's being so generous with? From what I've heard, until our Ernie won, big time, Ernest Craig was treated like a total pariah; like yesterday's dried dog shit! Nobody, but nobody would even bother to give him the proper time of day. Even that bleached cunt in the pub and that old codger who seems to spend his time there from dawn till dusk, sitting salivating over her, couldn't say a decent word!'

Ernest, meanwhile had also been visiting London for a weekly session with a makeover expert. Armed with his much-thumbed copy of Dale Carnegie's sure fire usurper of the Bible, How To Win Friends And Influence People (another courtesy of the loyal Miss Codlington) and with his lessons in personal etiquette and grooming, Ernest's long dormant, innate longing to become a male Eliza to her Higgins was – thanks to his unexpected good fortune – finally allowed to come to fruition. Ego and Id had, at long last, become the aforesaid Super Ego.

Ernest's dogged determination had seen the extraordinary transformation within himself taking only a few weeks as opposed to months. 'Each day The Rookery changes, Ernest B,' he would repeat to his alter ego, 'so do I!'

'Tell me about it?' would be the inevitable snapped reply. 'And Ernest A, would it be too much for your inflated ego to at least ask if I approve of whatever aftershave you happen to be dousing yourself at the present time. I loathe Hermes but adore Gucci!'

'Tough shit, Ernest B! And therefore, without any due consideration, I'm now going to give myself another spray of that Gucci Pour Homme! So, up yours, you old douche bag!'

'Fuck you!'

'You wish! Remember, I'm the one in dick control here!'

It happened several days later.

'Another cocktail party tonight at the Bridlington-Smythes, Ernest B.'

'Jesus! Ernest A! How much longer?

'Soon Ernest A and Ernest B! Very, very soon!' cut in Super Ego, who, while silently observing the two, bickering egos, had decided it time to intervene.

'Good!' muttered Ernest B., still scowling back at Ernest A. Continuing to ignore Super Ego, he suddenly changed tactic. Giving his doppelgänger a mischievous look he gave a derisive snort. 'Those fucking Bullshit-Smythes! Why you won't simply allow us to flash that massive cock of ours at one of their dreary receptions – like tonight – I simply don't know! Think of all those stunned faces!'

'Because, as I've said before, when push comes to wank, it's my dick we're talking about, even though you may have twenty four hour privy to it!' came the sharp rebuke. 'And no., Ernest B, I or we, don't flash! Too mundane! As Super Ego has just said, soon, very soon and I also know Super Ego can only agree – it's now payback time!' Here there was a theatrical pause. 'So, how about D Day, the Sixth of June, for our own little entertainment?'

'Sixth of June?' Again it was Super Ego speaking. 'I like it! I like it! Our planned landing but with a definite difference. No rescuing but a total reverse! As they say in filthy Frogland. Parfait!'

'About time too!' commented Doris Bridlington-Smythe, giving a disdainful sniff and handing an embossed invitation card across the breakfast table to a disinterested Peter B-S, heavily immersed in the Moorsfield Mail. 'Mister Ernest Craig is finally requesting the pleasure of our company!' She gave another sniff – this time a touch more dainty than disdainful. 'But no, we're not to be entertained in that monstrosity of a so-called cottage but at an outdoor soireé to welcome the start of the summer solstice!' Stretching to retrieve the invitation card – Peter had simply placed it face down on the table – she gave her husband a glare before loudly relaying the further information. 'We're all expected to gather on the village green at seven o'clock and from there our host will lead us to a Reckoning In The Woods! Reckoning? What on earth does the trumped up man mean by a Reckoning?'

'I reckon we just go along and find the fuck out!' came the surly reply from behind the paper.

Doris's curiosity was further whetted on learning that every member of the small village community, adults and children, had also been invited to partake in the mysterious event (apart from Miss Codlington who, so it seemed, was still circling the globe!).

Prior to the collection of their post by the various parties concerned – Hadlington didn't have a postman per se so everyone collected their own mail from Miss Hanson – the surprise bulk delivery of the twenty nine invitation cards to the village shop had only been previously usurped by Ernest arriving in a gleaming new Bentley Continental R coupè for one of his regular visits to view the work in progress on the site. It wasn't the luxurious car that caused the consternation but the fact that Ernest was the driver! The sight of Ernest 'behind the wheel' had, as Harriet Hanson was to frequently say, given her 'quite a turn!' However, the 'turn' was not sufficient to prevent her from adding. 'Must have been taking private lessons in Moorsfield. With all that money I'd have a uniformed chauffeur!'

Surrounded by the usual coterie in the Green Shepherd Harriet was able to divulge further information on the coming June event.

'He's having a special team up all the way from London,' she told the avid group of listeners. 'From what I can gather they're creating a folly in the woods!'

'Folly? What's a folly apart from a fucking mistake?' Reg gave a booming laugh at his flash of wit.

'A folly, if you don't mind,' said Hadlington's answer to Marie Antoinette (Paris Hilton duly forgotten), 'is a costly ornamental building, usually built for pleasure. Like that Brighton Pavillion!'

''Ark at her!' said Reg proudly. 'Fountain of knowledge, isn't she, my Cal?' Giving his blonde paramour a lewd wind he couldn't help adding. 'As far as I'm concerned our bedroom's our folly with me her personal fountain!'

'Tosser!' screeched Hadlington's Marie Antoinette.

'Dirty sod!' laughed Ted busily pouring another round 'on the house.'

The day after his winnings had been made public Ernest had stopped visiting the pub. Again, all the regulars were kept up to date with his several contributions for the benefit of the village. However it wasn't the benevolence of a new roof to the vicarage; the splendid new church organ and a new school hall that became the daily topics of conversation, but Ernest's apparent meanness.

'What's he doing with the rest?' had become a virtual rhetorical question.

'A day's interest alone on his lot would have easily covered those petty donations made,' sniped Harriet.

'He may look like a bloody millionaire with all his new finery but he's turned out to be nothing more than a sodding Scrooge,' was Dick aka Bull's-Eye Bill's opinion.

'Probably spending it all on some bit in that London town!' sniggered another of the group.

'I wonder what the bloke's name is?' chuckled Reg. 'Bummer?'

Loud laughter and shrieks accompanied this bon mot.

Contrary to their grizzling and disparaging comments concerning their host it was obvious that unless a major catastrophe occurred – Harriet had suggested the likes of an earthquake, a comment she would rue when it was too late – The Day Of Reckoning, as the event had been firmly christened, was one definitely not to be missed.

And, as with all anticipated happenings, the great day duly arrived.

Despite all endeavours by the likes of Bulls-eye Bill and Ted plus a few more curious locals attempting to get a sneak preview, the area for the party 'to end all parties' (Harriet Hanson's caustic yet fortuitous dubbing) had been securely kept under wraps from prying eyes.

'Bloody security guards and all!' grumbled Ted. 'Who the fuck does the guy think he is? The fucking Queen?'

Several vans (including a catering van) had arrived a week earlier and a team of workmen had spent at least six days setting up the folly. The men would arrive early each morning in a blacked out coach and depart later in the evening. At no stage was any contact made with any of the locals. The only snippet of information Harriet had been able to glean from a contact in Moorsfield itself was that the workmen had, literally, taken over the Holiday Inn.

'Dora says there must be at least thirty workmen. Thirty!' Such was her indignation that the woman forget to almost have one of her legendary turns.

Early on the morning of the sixth, two large catering vans had silently arrived and, as before, had been escorted by a silent, sullen man who appeared to be in charge of the whole event.

The day had dawned bright and clear. Even though she would be the last to admit it, even Doris Bridlington-Smythe could sense an air of excitement embracing Hadlington – or 'a frisson' as she so eloquently put it to Petah.

'More of a fucking fuck up!' had been the desultory reply.

While all had been summoned for seven o'clock, the first of the excited partygoers had begun to arrive well before the stipulated time ensuring the Green Shepherd an anticipated surge in orders. A wily Ted, assisted by Caroline, had spent a busy afternoon peeling and chopping fruit and preparing endless jugs of alcoholic Pimms. These were to be sold at a few pence each and it was not long before most of the happy imbibers were beginning to feel the effect. A special non alcoholic Pimms had also been supplied though most of the older children, led by the devious, raucous Dennis Carter, made sure that they too obtained their drinks from the regular jugs.

Unbeknown to the guests, apart from six handpicked men, all other works people and the caterers had already left via a new road that had been cut earlier through the woods leading both to and from the site. The installation of this second road had ensured the locals seeing only what they were expected to see; a few selected 'party' vans and subsequent coach arriving and making their and its' way through the village towards The Rookery.

'Good evening Hadlington!' At seven o'clock precisely, Ernest's voice – greatly exaggerated by a series of hidden amplifiers – suddenly boomed out from the direction of the church tower. Startled cries along with a few gasps and a few dropped glasses greeted the unexpected interruption. 'Welcome, welcome to my – Ernest Craig's – Rekoning! Now my dear ladies and gentlemen, teasing teenagers and dear little children, I need you to prepare yourselves for my big surprise. I am going to ask you to line up in pairs, two by two, exactly like those dear animals did for old Noah and his Ark! And once this is done, I am going lead you, rather like that naughty Pied Piper of Hamelin – remember him? – along past The Rookery and on to my fun party palace in the woods!' The disembodied voice paused for a moment to allow the buzz of excited conversation to rise to a crescendo. 'I promise you,' the loud voice boomed out again, 'I promise you a party to end all parties! And now, ladies and gentlemen, teasing teenagers and dear, dear sweet little children, I am not speaking from the church tower, in fact, I'm standing right behind you in front of the Green Shepherd!'

Turning and swirling to get a glimpse of their host, a cry went up at the sight of Ernest standing atop one of the outdoor tables belonging to the public house. And what a splendid sight this Super Ego presented to his already heady guests, intoxicated both by the excitement and the Pimms. Ernest, dressed in a loose white pierrot's clown costume, his face a blank white painted mask and his eyes appearing as two, deep glittering black pools set within their crosses of black vertical and horizontal lines, held – in one hand – a microphone and, in the other – a gleaming golden trumpet. Casting the microphone to the ground, he raised the trumpet towards his black painted lips but not before shouting 'A one a! A two a! A three a! A follow me a!' With that he blew a perfect high C note before launching into a startling rendition of the famous, uplifting Negro spiritual, When The Saints Go Marching In!

Without hesitation the happily laughing, jostling crowd, quickly assembled themselves into a straggly line of twos and threes, children in front while the smaller ones were hoisted onto their fathers' shoulders. Prancing and dancing alongside the eager queue, his trumpet emitting a never-ending flow of sweet, clear notes, Ernest aka Super Ego (Ernest A and Ernest B however, still there for the ride and much awaited final denouement), on reaching the front gave a 'follow me!' gesture with his free arm before setting along the road in the direction of The Rookery.

Passing this now splendid edifice set amidst its neatly trimmed lawns and carefully planted flowering shrubs, the happy partygoers followed their energetic, trumpeting host along the newly gravelled and flower festooned road deep into the mysterious woods ending up in an enormous glade where, to their amazement, stood a perfect wooden replica of an elaborate dome being part of the gaudy Regency Pavillion as commissioned at the start of the 19th century by the Prince Regent, later George 1V, and set in the seaside spa of Brighton.

Cries of 'oohs, aahs' and a few more explicit 'fucks' to the more personal 'fuck me!' greeted the amazing sight. Still playing the seductive Saints a super-charged Ernest dancingly led them through a large set of double doors into the large wooden rotunda.

Inside, the cries of amazement grew with ever increasing enthusiasm at the sight of the vast, dome swathed in brightly coloured silks along with matching wall hangings and floral wreaths. A vast buffet and bar had been set up at one side of the encased area while a series of exquisitely silk covered tables, surrounded by glistening gold painted chairs and decorated again with a central wreath of flowers, elaborate glowing candelabra and sparkling silver cutlery, all adding to the breathtaking vision. Lively piped organ music now took over from Ernest's energetic trumpeting thus continuing the feel of general bonhomie. Six silent pierrot figures – though these wore loose black silk costumes in strong contrast to Ernest's white – moved smoothly between the happy guests serving them silver goblets filled with a bright pink concoction.

Had a festive parent taken the time to look at her child she would have noticed that the children, as well as the adults, were being served the same concoction but in fun plastic beakers in the form of a deadpan pierrot's head. (At this stage of the proceeding it would do well to remember that the total population of Hadlington, including the children, numbered only some forty souls making up the fifteen families).

It was about an hour later that Doris Bridlington-Smythe happened to notice not only the absence of the black clad pierrots but also the white costumed Ernest. Glancing casually over an animated Harriet Hanson''s shoulder towards a giggling Caroline and Reg, she also noted, to her alarm, several of the children slumped in their various chairs and staring dazedly into space. 'Harriet...' she began to say when she too found herself overcome by a dizzying spell. Shaking her head she glanced wildly at Harriet who, her own eyes widening, suddenly appeared to visibly crumple before falling slowly down on to the polished wood strip floor. Shaking her head more vigorously in an effort to clear her vision she was suddenly deafened by the change in the music. From the toe tapping show tunes (several couples were seen to suddenly stumble on the small, central dance floor) the music blasted into Chopin's Funeral March.

'I need air! I need air!' Doris gasped, her voice rising in panic. Almost tripping over the recumbent Harriet she staggered across towards a now gaping Reg and Caroline where a fast moving Reg just managed to catch her inside his brawny arms. 'What's happening? What's happening?' she chokingly asked the bewildered man (Caroline now also clutching wildly at her lover's other arm). 'The noise! (the organ music had now reached an ear-splitting crescendo). 'Oh my God!' Doris Bridlington-Smythe gave a scream to end all screams. 'Fire!'

With a shaking finger the swaying, shaking woman pointed at a smouldering, silk-draped wall which suddenly burst into rampant tongues of bright yellow and red flames. As if in a well rehearsed routine, similar tongues of flame appeared at regular intervals around the vast rotunda. Within seconds the elaborately tented ceiling itself burst into a violent roar of turbulent fire.

Screams and wails of panic were simply drowned out by the blaring Funeral March blaring out from the hidden speakers. More screams – this time even louder than the thundering organ music – came when a few, having managed to reach the huge double doors – found them firmly bolted shut. The one and only exit had earlier been unknowingly closed and bolted by the quietly departing Ernest and his six cronies.

Amidst further screams of 'We're trapped! And 'Get me out of here!' there came another piercing shriek. 'The floor! The floor! My God, what's happening with the floor?'

'Jesus!' bellowed a red-faced Peter Bridlington-Smythe as he found his feet voluntarily separating from each other as a rapidly opening line began to quickly bisect the floor displaying the deep, green slime of the swamp beneath. Before he could regain his balance the heavily set man fell backwards into the engulfing muck beneath the rotunda. By now it was total panic as the widening gap saw tables and more bodies falling into the ever growing marshy opening. Those who found themselves pushed together on the rapidly dwindling surface were soon forced back into the swamp or found themselves engulfed in flaming fabric. As if choreographed to a perfection it was then the burning wooden roof of the dome collapsed onto the remaining few screaming, sobbing families. One of the last figures to finally succumb to the pile of burning wood and fabric before sinking into the greedily receptive swamp was a determinedly struggling, yelling teenage Dennis Carter whose day of reckoning had – unfortunately for him – appeared to have arrived several decades too early. The boy's battle for survival was nothing short of awesome.

Two hours later, apart from a few charred stumps left sticking out from the now placid surface of the swamp, all signs of the former folly and the inhabitants of Hadlington had completely disappeared.

It was a full two days later before a visitor passing through the village and deciding to stop for a drink, had entered the deserted Green Shepherd public house. His curiosity aroused he had then noticed the complete silence surrounding the equally deserted village green. Any evidence of the former revelry had been cleared away by Ernest and his team of pierrots on their return to Hadlington. Having bolted the doors to the dome, offset the synchronised electrical coils to start the fires and set the hydraulics to the moveable platform in motion, the clean up to the green had been quietly and efficiently carried out. But it was the eerie stillness and emptiness of the village which could not be explained. Returning to his car the now decidedly nervous visitor had collected his mobile and called 999.

In due course the swamp would be drained and the charred remains of the former inhabitants discovered. Adding to the mystery was the discovery of a vast, portable hydraulic system which, when reassembled, turned out to be part of a burnt out dual wooden platform able to have been opened and closed like the jaws of a giant whale. Identification of the various families proved almost impossible. The lavish Petit Trianon or Petit Versailles, the dream home of the three Ernest's, Ego, Id and Super Ego, was to remain deserted and gradually returned to its former derelict state.

Craig Hadlington as he is now known (the three egos had finally come to accept that three is a crowd and two were no longer required) lives in hedonistic splendour outside Cape Town in South Africa. Making up for the missing number two is a gentle, grey-haired elderly woman whom Craig proudly introduces as his great aunt. Unlike Ernest and his three former egos, his so-called aunt has retained her maiden name of Codlington.

Finally, one should not forget a very regular young visitor to Pied Piper, the elegant estate owned by Craig and set near to Groote Schuur, the legendary gabled Dutch homestead, once the home of Cecil Rhodes. The young man – almost considered a member of the family and perhaps even the substitute number three – had originally been introduced to Craig and Miss Codlington at a braaivleis (the local name for a barbecue) held by a friendly neighbour. Perhaps it is only the strangest of coincidences that the atrociously scarred loner (it was later revealed he had been badly burned in a hideous car accident) is named Dennis.

ABOUT THE AUTHOR

Robin Anderson, an internationally known author and interior designer was born in Scotland and brought up in the former Southern Rhodesia (now Zimbabwe) and South Africa. Before attending Rhodes University (the Oxford of South Africa) he hosted his own radio programme in Rhodesia ('The Golden Voice of Teenage Half Hour!) and worked as a cub reporter on 'The Bulawayo Chronicle' during his gap year.

Leaving South Africa, he spent the early Sixties working with interior design companies in Paris, New York and London. He set up his own design company in London in 1970. Although interior design had been his first interest, the designer never stopped writing. Nowadays he makes numerous television appearances and is a regular guest on selected radio programmes, gives regular lectures on his writing.

His first novel, REGINA, A NOVEL OF SOME EXTREMES, was published in 1998. The novel gives a salacious look 'behind the scenes' of the glamorous but bitchy and competitive world of interior design, following the path of the unpleasant but talented Reginald Forbes as he cuts a swathe through the lives of his many unsuspecting victims.

Though London-based, the author travels extensively and the benefits of this are apparent in the various settings to his books. The Amazon, the Yucatan, Borneo, Myanmar, China, Russia, Japan, Sri Lanka, India, Egypt, Morocco, Kenya, Australia, The Maldives, Mauritius, Central Europe, Canada, North and South America plus the majority of the Caribbean Islands have also been visited. He has walked the Inca Trail in Peru; climbed Mount Kinabulu (Borneo) and Mount Kilimanjaro (Tanzania).

The author is a strong believer in the protection of endangered species. In 1959 he took part in 'Operation Noah' which involved the rescue of hundreds of animals from the rising waters of the new Kariba Dam being across the mighty Zambezi River in the north/western part of Zimbabwe.

He is also the proud 'foster parent' to four Orang-utans living at the famous Orang-utan Sanctuary in Sepilok, Borneo plus two elephants, Marlene and Marlon, who live happily on a ranch in Zimbabwe.

In a total contrast to the above, he also helped with the salvaging of precious works of art and manuscripts in Florence, Italy, during the Sixties when the Rover Arno burst its banks and flooded a major part of the ancient city.

In between his travels Anderson lives mainly in a spacious studio 'overlooking a glorious, leafy square' in London's exclusive Chelsea and a small hideaway in the Cinque Terre in his beloved Italy.

'Have laptop, will write and will travel!' is his mantra. *Thirteen Tales of Textual Arousal* is his seventh novel.

ROBIN ANDERSON 2010
www.robin-anderson.com

A NOVEL BY
ROBIN ANDERSON

ANDERSON

STILL LIFE

STILL
LIFE

A
BONER
BOOK

www.ingramcontent.com/pod-product-compliance
Lightning Source LLC
Chambersburg PA
CBHW051148260626
47170CB00005B/2007